121 Pudding Street

Books by Jean Fritz

121 PUDDING STREET
FISH HEAD

121
PUDDING
STREET

by Jean Fritz

ILLUSTRATED BY SOFIA

Coward-McCann, Inc.
New York

To my Mother and Father

121 Pudding Street

Chapter 1

AT ONE end of Pudding Street there were six white houses and an empty lot. This was the busy end of the street. Front doors were continually slamming behind someone running out with a base-ball bat, roller skates, or a peanut butter sandwich.

All the boys and girls, cats and dogs, lived at this end of the street. All the noise started around the six white houses, rolled up and down the sidewalks, spread into back yards, and, more often than not, spilled into the empty lot.

At the other end of Pudding Street there was one gray house, Number 121. It stood stiff and alone, closed off from the rest of the world by a high wooden fence.

"What a waste!" Mary thought for the thousandth time as she roller-skated slowly up to the gate in the wooden fence. It was a slatted gate, much lower than the fence itself, and the only place where one could get a full-length view of the house.

Mary shook her head. Half of Pudding Street lay

wasted around that wrinkled old house. And a perfectly good tree, too. She couldn't see the tree from the gate, but she had seen it before often enough, from the empty lot. They had all studied it through the knothole in the fence that separated the empty lot from Number 121. They couldn't see too much of the tree, but they had seen enough to make one thing certain. It was a good climbing tree and it was wasted.

Mary sighed and skated on. Even roller skates sounded especially noisy here where it was always so quiet. It wasn't a happy quiet, either. It was a cold quiet, Mary decided as she reached the end of the street and turned around to come back.

But again when she reached the gate, she stopped. She always hoped that somehow the house might have mysteriously improved in her absence. But there was no change. The house was the same as before, the same as always—its windows closed, every shade pulled tight. Not even a drop of sunlight could possibly leak into it.

"I bet the curtains in that house have never had a chance to dance in the breeze," Mary thought and it made her feel sad, particularly on such a perfect day as this, with school just out for the summer. Not even a house had a right to look so dingy and silent today.

"It's just a wrinkled, old, dried-up, dark thing,"

Mary declared and she started to skate away. "It's like a—"

Mary hesitated. She always liked to find the right word for everything. What was the right word for the gray house?

"Like a wrinkled, dried-up—raisin." The word popped out unexpectedly and Mary smiled. It was right. "Like a raisin on Pudding Street."

Mary repeated it several times and it kept on sounding right. Suddenly it gave her an idea. She pointed her finger at the gray house and grinned.

"Number 121, you are going to have a surprise," she said out loud.

Mary speeded up her skates and went screeching down the street. She turned in at one of the white houses, kicked off her skates, and disappeared inside.

In a moment she was back and blowing a whistle —three short blasts and one long. The effect was immediate. First of all, the dog, Creep-up, and the cat, Mashed Potato, pounded into the yard. On Pudding Street whistles sometimes meant refreshments.

The boys and girls came next, screen doors slamming behind them. Timothy was the oldest and the best hedge jumper but, even so, he arrived only two sneaker lengths ahead of Jane and her flying pigtails. Christopher was slowed down by a coke bottle which, as usual, he had to finish before he could start anything else. Patrick, the cowboy of the group, could be heard long before he was seen. His *yippee ky-otes* went ahead of him and with him, and echoed behind him as he galloped up to Mary's house on his make-believe horse, Lickety.

Everyone moved over to make room for Patrick and Lickety. Make-believe or not, Lickety took up quite a bit of space, and the others had learned long ago through bitter experience with Patrick that it didn't pay to ignore Lickety or walk carelessly through him.

The last one to arrive was Ann. She was five years old and the youngest one on the street, but that had nothing to do with her being late. Usually Ann was right there with the others. Today she kept stopping along the way to dress Lisa. Lisa was Ann's doll and had to go everywhere Ann went—unless, Ann explained, she could find a doll-sitter.

At last Lisa was ready, and Ann trotted up the sidewalk, her eyes bright with anticipation. Even though she had only recently been allowed in on Pudding Street Plans, Ann knew what the "come-on-over" whistle meant. Almost always it started off a new Plan, and on Pudding Street, Plans were important. Sometimes it would be a Plan for a picnic. Sometimes a Plan for a game or a play or a lemonade stand. Once the whistle had started off a Plan for a circus in the empty lot and Ann had dressed up as a lion tamer. Ann plumped down on the bottom step of the porch now and waited.

"I have an idea," Mary announced mysteriously as soon as she saw that everyone was there. "It's a party idea."

"Goody!" Ann bounced Lisa happily on her lap.

"Sounds all right," Christopher approved, sucking loudly at the last drops of coke in his bottle. "What kind of a party?"

Mary dropped her voice dramatically. "A christening," she said.

"Sounds even better," Christopher nodded.

Every new cat, every new doll, every goldfish on Pudding Street, had been christened at a party. Mary usually thought of the names because she liked to write poetry and was good at that sort of thing. Then they had elaborate name-giving ceremonies followed by refreshments.

"Who has anything new?" Patrick asked.

"No one," Mary replied. "We are going to christen something old. We're going to christen the gray house. I have a name for it—the Raisin. The Raisin of Pudding Street."

There was a moment of surprised silence while they all thought it over. A house! They had never named a house before.

"The Raisin." Christopher repeated it experimentally and then shook his head. "Sounds too sweet. Sour Grapes would be more like it. Or the Persimmon."

Jane sighed loudly. "Mary is not talking about the taste of the house," she countered. "She is talking about the looks. If you took your mind off food for a few minutes, Christopher, you would see clearly enough that the gray house looks exactly like a dried-up raisin."

Christopher grunted. "All right, call it the Raisin, then," he agreed. "But how are you going to christen it? You can't go about it like you do with a doll or a cat. How can you sprinkle a house?"

"I know," Patrick shouted, jumping up and down. "I know how to do it! We can squirt the gray house. With water pistols. Right over the fence we can squirt it."

Mary smiled. It wasn't a bad idea. But when she looked at Timothy, she could see that it wasn't the idea they were going to use.

Timothy was leaning against the porch railing, looking as if he had just struck gold. He tipped his sailor cap over his right eye and grinned.

"You don't sprinkle," he said. "And you don't squirt. You christen a house the way you christen a ship. You crash. With a bottle."

Timothy was the sailor of the group. He was always making boats, reading boat books, talking boat talk. Sometimes it was pretty boring, but now it sounded like fun—even to Cowboy Patrick who had no use for the sea.

"You take a bottle of pop," Timothy went on eagerly. "You crash it against the side of the house. Wham! It spills all over and breaks into a million pieces. At the same time you give the house its name."

"What do you mean, the bottle *spills?*" Christopher demanded. "You wouldn't waste a full bottle, for the love of Pete! What's the matter with an empty one?"

"No," Timothy answered positively. "We're going to do this *right*. Period. When you christen anything, it's got to get wet. You know that much, Chris."

"Does it have to be pop?" Christopher groaned.

15

"What's the matter with filling an empty bottle with water?"

Christopher's scowl looked so threatening that Mary blew her whistle to stall off any more argument.

"Who thought of the name, anyway?" she demanded. "*I* did. And *I* say—do it right, the way Timothy says."

She took out the pencil and pad she always carried with her, and wrote carefully across the top of the paper, NOTES FOR CHRISTENING. Under this, she wrote: 1. Method—by bottle.

They all crowded together behind Mary and looked over her shoulder. Plans always seemed more definite and important once Mary started to write them down. But instead of putting down "2," Mary hesitated. How could she go ahead? she wondered. In fact, how could they go ahead with the christening plans at all?

"Come on, come on," Patrick urged impatiently, but Jane motioned him to be quiet.

"How can she go on?" Jane said as if she had read Mary's thoughts. She turned to Timothy. "And how do you expect to crash a bottle against a house somebody lives in?" she asked coldly. "Just what are you going to do about Miss Pursey?"

"Yes," Mary echoed, "what about Miss Pursey?"

It wasn't as if anyone could really forget Miss

Pursey. They all knew that she lived in the gray house. But she seldom made any difference in their plans, one way or another. Except for the tree. They would have liked a try at climbing that tree in her back yard, but if they had asked her, she would just have poked her head out the door and said No.

Miss Pursey always said No—that is, when she bothered to say anything. On Halloween she didn't bother. She locked up everything lockable and then hired Mr. Shift to stand all evening outside the gate. If he fell asleep—and he always did—Miss Pursey was much too far inside to know the difference. She was always so far inside, that it was sometimes hard to believe anyone lived in the gray house at all.

Day in and day out, not even the position of a shade changed except for those few times when Mr. Shift appeared in his car to act as Miss Pursey's chauffeur for an afternoon. Then, and then only, would the house come creaking back to life. An upstairs shade would snap up, a door would jerk open, and there would be Miss Pursey. Looking neither to the right nor to the left, she would blow out like a stiff breeze on an unpleasant bit of duty. When she returned, the gray house would close tightly around her and Pudding Street might not see her again for weeks.

But she would be there. And how could they plan a decent christening with Miss Pursey around? If they asked her permission or invited her to the christening, she would simply stick her nose out of the door and say No.

Still, it was such a good idea, Timothy couldn't give it up yet. He frowned and moved restlessly around the porch. "There must be some way," he said.

Patrick shot off his gun to help everyone think. "Maybe we could be so quiet she wouldn't hear us," he suggested.

"Fat chance with you around," muttered Timothy. He looked meaningfully at Patrick, who had a gun in each hand and a third one sticking out of a hip pocket. "First thing you know Miss Pursey would have Mr. Shift guarding the gate all the time."

At the mention of Mr. Shift, Jane snapped her fingers.

"I've got it!" she exclaimed. "When Mr. Shift comes, Miss Pursey . . . goes . . . out." Jane spoke slowly so that her meaning would be clear.

Even so, for a moment nobody understood. Christopher was the first to catch on. "I get it," he said with a grin. "We'll do it while she's out. There'll be plenty of time."

Mary took out her notebook again.

"2," she wrote. "Time—when Miss Pursey is out."

Timothy settled his cap on the back of his head.

"3," he dictated. "Preparation." He cleared his throat importantly and went on in a captain kind of voice. "Under this, we will list the order in which we stand watch."

"Stand watch?" Mary repeated blankly. "What for?"

"To see when Miss Pursey goes out," Timothy explained. "It will be just like a ship. We'll take turns watching for Mr. Shift's car. It will probably be days until he comes, and we'll have plenty of time to get ready. But when he comes, we'll have to act quickly."

"Order of Watch," Mary wrote down.

"Me first!" Patrick shouted. "Write my name down. Me first! Me!" He pulled at Mary's arm and poked Timothy in the ribs to get his attention.

"All right, all right," Timothy agreed hastily. "Go on—right now. Take the first two hours. Fire your gun if there is any sign of Mr. Shift."

"And that's the *only* time you fire a gun," Jane called as Patrick swaggered up the street with all three dogs at his heels. Lickety followed on an invisible lead rope.

"Now maybe we can do our planning in peace," Mary sighed as she put Patrick's name down at the top of the Order of Watch.

"And get down to important matters," Christopher added. "Such as . . . refreshments. If you are thinking of appointing a committee of one to round up some tasty morsels for the christening, I would be . . . ah . . . glad—"

"To be chairman," Mary finished for him. Christopher's mind was like a refrigerator, she thought. Every time it opened up, all you could see was food.

"Why, I'd be glad to be chairman," Christopher agreed as if he hadn't thought of the idea himself. "First I'll make a house-to-house check on supplies. Starting right now. Best to be prepared, you know." He thumped his stomach and dashed off.

As soon as Christopher had gone, Timothy plunged into plans for the official ceremony. "We'll have speeches and flags and singing, but the most important part, of course, will be the bottle-breaking."

"In the movies a girl always breaks the bottle," Mary reminded him, "so I should do it. I thought of the name."

"I want to break it," Ann cried. "I like to break things."

Jane pointed out that she was the oldest girl and ought to have some privileges.

"Crum!" Timothy muttered. All the time he had been counting on breaking the bottle himself. Well, maybe they could work it out some way. Maybe they could all do it. If they used a lot of bottles, there would be a bigger crash. That might be even better. But Timothy's thoughts were suddenly interrupted.

BANG

It couldn't be. There must be some mistake. Patrick couldn't be giving the signal—not so soon.

Timothy uncoiled himself from the porch railing. Everyone listened intently.

There the noise went again.

In one leap Timothy was down all three porch steps. "If that kid is just playing cowboy games," he growled, racing up the street, "I'll throw him in the brig and put him on bread and water."

Jane, Mary, and Ann followed at Timothy's heels. Christopher came running from across the street. The closer they came to the gray house, the clearer it was that Patrick was not playing games. He was in a froth of excitement. He was jumping up and down, jerking his head backward, rolling his eyes, and waving his elbows.

Timothy looked behind Patrick in the direction his elbows were waving. There, shivering by the curb, was Mr. Shift's black car with Mr. Shift, himself, slumped sleepily over the wheel.

Then, as if he had just remembered where he was, he leaned lazily on the horn of his car. The horn made only a weak gurgle, but that was enough. Almost immediately Miss Pursey burst from the house and out to the car. She was wearing a black hat with a long, stiff feather in the front that pointed straight up like a knife. When she ducked her head to get into the car, the knife pointed straight at Mr. Shift. He didn't even seem to notice. He continued to nod sleepily over the wheel and started up the car as if he were still in a dream.

Timothy kept his eyes on Miss Pursey's feather as the car jerked off and disappeared down the street. Timothy sighed with relief. Miss Pursey had gone.

But now what? What was the next step? Should they go ahead with their plans?

Timothy considered. Of course, they were not ready to go ahead, but they would be taking a chance if they didn't. Miss Pursey might not go out again for weeks. Maybe not all summer.

"Let's go!" he cried. "We'll start the program in twenty minutes."

Before anyone knew quite what was happening, he was rattling off orders and sending his crew scurrying in all directions. Jane was off to find a flag and flagpole. Mary disappeared to write a poem in honor of the Raisin. Christopher was to finish rounding up the refreshments, and Ann went to collect her dolls so there would be a big audience for the christening. Patrick was left on watch, with instructions to fire a gun in twenty minutes.

Timothy set himself the job of making a platform. He found an old orange crate in his cellar. The only trouble was, it looked like an orange crate. Black letters on one side said KISSED BY THE SUN, and on the other side FLORIDA'S SWEETEST. He couldn't stand up on a platform like that, and there wasn't time to paint it.

Then Timothy remembered the red crepe paper in the attic left over from Christmas. Quickly he ran up the stairs and brought down the Christmas box. He tacked the crepe paper around the crate and, as a final touch on the front, he added a silver star. When he stepped back to inspect the platform, he had to admit it looked fine. Rather fancy, in fact.

Timothy picked up the platform and rushed back to the gray house. He passed Patrick, who was so busy looking at his watch he didn't look up. As Timothy reached the gate, he slowed down. He just couldn't run through that gate as if it were something he did every day. Well, he didn't need to hurry. There was plenty of time. Maybe there would even be time after the christening to take a look at that tree behind the house. As Timothy went into the yard, he wondered if anyone else had thought of the tree.

If they had, they didn't say so. Jane and Mary were busy helping Ann seat her dolls in three even rows. Timothy set up his platform in front of them and was about to step onto it when out on the sidewalk Patrick pulled his trigger.

Time was up.

"Come on," Timothy urged the girls. "We begin on the sidewalk."

They lined up in front of the gate—all but Christopher. He came puffing up at the last minute behind two enormous paper bags of refreshments. Under his arm he carried his bugle.

Timothy grinned. It was going to be a good christening. He swung open the gate and led the procession in—boys, girls, Creep-up, Mashed Potato, and Lickety. Patrick let Lickety loose to graze as the rest took their places quietly behind the doll audience. Only Creep-up lingered a little longer at the gate. But that was to be expected. Creep-up was a dog who could never bear to part with a smell once he had found it.

Christopher stepped onto the platform first and blew an opening bugle call. Patrick followed, firing three shots from each of his three guns. Jane planted a broomstick flagpole in the ground with a flag waving from the top.

"Salute to the flag!" Timothy called.

They saluted. They sang "The Star-Spangled Banner." They sang "Anchors Aweigh." Then Timothy climbed up onto the platform to make a speech.

"Ladies and gentlemen—" he began.

Everyone sat up straight. Five minutes later, when he had finished, they gave him a standing cheer. And they clapped so thunderously when Timothy left the platform that there was nothing for him to do but come back and dance a sailor's hornpipe.

Mary was next on the program. She stood on the platform and pulled out her notebook with the poem she had written. She began to read in her special

poetry voice, louder and higher than her normal voice.

> All of you who are here
>   Please listen.
> Now is the time for us
>   To christen
> A house which for years has had
>   No name
> But today is covered with glory
>   And fame.
> It is for this very reason
>   We meet
> To name you . . . *Raisin of*
>   *Pudding Street.*

Mary sat down amid such a round of approval that she wished she had written two poems. But there was no time to think about that now.

The grand moment had arrived. It was time for the bottle-breaking.

"How many bottles did you get?" Timothy whispered.

"Eleven." Christopher grinned. "Some of us can have seconds."

"Good." Timothy nodded. "We can all crash." He began to pass bottles around.

Christopher's eyes bulged. "All?" he asked weakly. "You mean crash more than one bottle?"

The others were taking bottles and lining up along the front of the house.

Christopher put his bottle firmly back in the bag. "Not me," he said. "I'm not crashing." And he turned his back as Timothy began the count.

"Ready, get set—

CRASH

"In the name of Pudding Street," Timothy shouted, "I name you *Raisin!*"

Guns, whistles, barks, exploded all at once. Christopher couldn't bear not being part of the uproar. He picked up his bugle and played "Yankee Doodle" from beginning to end.

Grape pop dribbled down the front of the house. Orange pop and lime pop trickled down and mixed in it. (Christopher made it a point not to look.) Ann, who had christenings and weddings mixed up, had started to scatter a box of rice over the lawn when a shivering noise sounded out in the street. No one heard it. Timothy had just organized a snake dance when the gate was flung open.

No one noticed that. Patrick had just discovered he could make up poetry, too. He was dancing around in a little circle by himself.

"Mercy, mercy on Miss Pursey," he sang. "Mercy, mercy—"

He almost bumped into Jane. She was standing absolutely still, looking toward the gate, and there was a funny expression on her face.

All of a sudden everyone knew.

She was back.

Chapter 2

THE SNAKE dance stopped dead.

So did Miss Pursey. In one terrible, sweeping glance, Miss Pursey saw the children, the animals, the rice, the splattered house. Then slowly, without saying a word, her eyes began to travel again over the scene as if this time she meant to fix each awful detail in her mind and never forget it.

As Jane followed Miss Pursey's gaze, she cringed. It *did* look as if a carnival had been dumped in Miss

Pursey's front yard. But the mess would be easy to clean up. Jane wanted to cry out that it would only take ten minutes to put everything right but she was stopped by Miss Pursey's face. It loomed over her like something out of a nightmare. And every minute it seemed to grow more frightening. "She looks as if she's getting ready to be the witch in Hansel and Gretel," Jane thought desperately, wishing she knew how to change Miss Pursey's face back again.

It was at this moment that Patrick and Mary turned and ran out of the gate. Ann must have gone too, Jane thought, because she wasn't in sight. Jane moved closer to Timothy and Christopher, who stood shuffling their feet in a pool of rice. She nudged Timothy to do something but Timothy only shuffled harder.

Jane took a deep breath. "Please, Miss Pursey," she said, "we were just christening your house. We were going to clean up the mess. The pop stains will wash off in the rain and we'll pick up all the glass and rice."

Jane looked closely to see if Miss Pursey's face had improved.

It hadn't.

"Mr. Shift," Miss Pursey shrieked and her face seemed to crack. "Mr. Shift!"

Timothy tried. "Please, Miss Pursey," he began, "we'll fix everything." He leaned over and began to scoop up rice with both hands and stuff it into his pockets. Christopher dropped to his knees to help. So did Jane.

It was a relief to be doing something, Jane thought, instead of just standing and looking at Miss Pursey. She became so intent on filling the pockets of her blue jeans with rice that she didn't notice anything else. She didn't see Miss Pursey approaching until all at once—there was her shadow, black as a thundercloud, lying in front of Jane.

The shadow of Miss Pursey was almost more frightening than Miss Pursey herself. It stretched Miss Pursey out even longer and skinnier than she really was. Jane shivered. She didn't dare look up, even when Miss Pursey started to talk.

"Mr. Shift!" Miss Pursey called in a voice so shrill that even her shadow seemed to shrink back. *"Get these creatures out of here."*

Suddenly Jane didn't feel frightened any more. When someone called you a "creature," you couldn't go on feeling frightened. You were too mad.

Jane stood up slowly, dropping rice in two little streams to the ground.

"You don't need to bother about Mr. Shift," she said haughtily. "We are leaving anyway."

Jane walked over to the broomstick flagpole, taking care on the way to step hard on the shadow of Miss Pursey's head. Jane jerked the flagpole out of the ground and clapped it on her shoulder. She scooped up Ann's dolls in both arms and stalked out

31

of the yard, her braids hanging straight as two exclamation points. Christopher followed with the bugle and remaining pop bottles, and Timothy with the platform.

Creep-up, of course, was the last to go. He was taking a final whiff of that gate smell as Miss Pursey swept into the house and slammed the door. He was still smelling when Mr. Shift shuffled up the walk.

"Dogs, cats, kids—" Mr. Shift muttered to himself. "Pity they couldn't have waited a few weeks." His eyes, small and black as watermelon seeds, darted unhappily around the yard. They might have passed over Creep-up altogether if he had stayed where he was. But at just that moment Creep-up discovered that the gate smell continued in a narrow track toward the Raisin.

"Here, Creep-up," Timothy called desperately from the gate. "Here, boy."

Creep-up wagged his tail at Timothy to show that he heard, but his nose was to the ground and he wouldn't turn back.

Mr. Shift glared as Creep-up snuffled across the grass. "S-s-s-," Mr. Shift began. "S-s- SCAT!"

Creep-up sat down hard on the ground. Scat, indeed! That was the way to talk to cats. He began to warm up a growl, starting it off deep and fierce in his chest. He had just got it rolling well when Timothy dashed back and grabbed his collar.

"There, boy, there," Timothy murmured and

dragged him, still grumbling, to the empty lot where the others were gathered by the fence. Patrick had his eye at a knothole.

"What's happening?" Timothy asked.

"Nothing," Patrick replied shortly. "Not a thing since you and Creep-up left."

And for the next few minutes, nothing did happen. Mr. Shift, too, had disappeared into the house. Timothy dropped to the ground with his back against the fence.

"What a day!" he sighed. He let his mind drift back over the episode with Mr. Shift and Creep-up. Mr. Shift was certainly an odd character, Timothy thought—always mumbling to himself. What was it Mr. Shift had been mumbling about when he came in the gate? It had sounded as if he said, "Pity they couldn't have waited." Waited for what? Timothy shook his head; it didn't make sense. But then, not much that happened at 121 did make sense.

"Will you look at that!" Patrick shouted. Timothy wiggled over to the knothole and Patrick made room for him to take a look.

Timothy put his eye up to the hole and blinked. Mr. Shift and Miss Pursey were coming out of the Raisin, their arms full of chairs. They put them down at the front gate and Mr. Shift walked out, closing the gate behind him. Immediately Miss Pursey went to work. Timothy could see her face, set like a stone, as she pushed chairs against the gate.

She braced them. She put rocks against the chair legs. She piled chairs on top of each other. It took several trips and more chairs to satisfy Miss Pursey but at last she went into the Raisin and didn't come out again.

"She's built herself a regular fort," Timothy grunted. "Only thing she needs now is a rifle. She ought to sit behind those chairs with a rifle across her knees, ready for Indians."

"Maybe I could lend her one," Patrick said and then remembered that he was one of the Indians! He changed his tune quickly. "She better not point a rifle at me," he shouted. "I'd shoot it right out of her hand. Right through the knothole I'd shoot—bing!—like this—"

Patrick tried to stick the muzzle of his gun into the knothole but Christopher was there now and wouldn't move.

"Like this—" Patrick tried again.

"Drop dead," Christopher said, standing firm. "If you've got to do something, why don't you take a look out in front and see what old Shuffle-toes Shift is up to?"

Patrick stopped pushing Christopher and listened.

"It sounds like hammering," he said.

"Yea," Christopher agreed. "If you were quiet long enough, you might hear something."

Patrick was already off—around the fence to the sidewalk.

When he came back, his eyes were wide. "He's putting up a padlock," he reported. "At least, I think it's a padlock. Come and look."

Timothy shook his head. "Later. When Mr. Shift has gone. I've had enough of that guy for one day." Creep-up moved close to Timothy and wagged his tail.

"You know," Christopher remarked thoughtfully as they all sat down to wait for Mr. Shift to leave, "I don't believe—" Christopher frowned and shook his head as if he had just reached a weighty conclusion. "I don't believe that Miss Pursey likes us."

"Why, Christopher," Jane said in a voice that pretended to sound surprised, "whatever gave you that idea?"

Over at the knothole Patrick grunted in disgust. At least when he talked, what he said made sense. Bang—he fired his gun through the knothole.

"Someday all your noise is going to land you in a nest of trouble." Christopher was on his way to the sidewalk with the others, and poked Patrick as he passed. Patrick turned around. There was Mr. Shift's car, sputtering past the empty lot and on down Pudding Street.

Patrick dropped his gun into his holster and rushed to the gate, pushing past everyone else. "Sure, it's a padlock. A whopper." He shook the lock and tried to pry it open. "Won't open, either."

"Of course not." Timothy didn't need to try it to

know it wouldn't open. It was a padlock as big as a man's fist. "We're locked out now for sure," he said. "Padlock on one side, barricade on the other."

"Yep," Christopher agreed quickly. "Nothing more to do here." And, of course, everyone could see that he was right.

Christopher led the way back to the empty lot. He walked directly to the paper bags he had left with the other christening equipment beside the fence.

"My friends," he announced, stepping up onto the platform. "We continue with the christening ceremony. The house has been named and now the best part of the afternoon has arrived. We eat."

He jumped down from the platform and reached into the first paper bag. As he handed an orange pop to Mary, he did some fast figuring. There had been eleven bottles. Five had been crashed. That left six —one bottle apiece. He handed out bottles, making sure to save a lime pop for himself.

But when he pulled out his bottle, it wasn't lime at all. It was grape. Christopher frowned. Something had gone wrong. He was sure he had saved a lime. He reached in again and brought out another bottle. This one was lime, all right, but what about the extra grape bottle? Had his figuring been wrong? No, an extra bottle could mean only one thing. Someone must be missing. Christopher looked around.

"Where's Ann?" he asked.

Where was she? She hadn't been listening at the fence with them. She hadn't run away from Miss Pursey when Mary and Patrick had. Then Jane remembered that she hadn't seen Ann since the snake dance.

"She must have hidden when Miss Pursey came back," she said. *"She must still be at the Raisin!"*

"And she doesn't even know she's locked in!" Timothy groaned. "What if she goes to the gate and finds all that stuff piled there? What will she do?"

"She'll howl," Jane declared flatly. "You know Ann. You know she'll howl."

"And yell," Christopher agreed, sucking up the last of his pop.

"And scream," added Mary.

This was certainly Trouble with a capital T. In the first place, the fence was too high for even Timothy to climb easily, and in the second place, who at this particular moment was eager to be seen on the top of Miss Pursey's fence? Still, the grim fact remained that Ann must be warned. She must be rescued before she did anything to bring out Miss Pursey.

Christopher dug the heel of his shoe angrily into the ground. If *he'd* been doing it, he thought, this wouldn't have happened. There wouldn't have been any broken bottles. There wouldn't have been any mess. He turned crossly to Timothy.

37

"O.K., Captain, what do we do now?" Christopher demanded. "We are at sea; the radio has failed. You need to send a message."

Timothy grinned. "Well, Chris," he said calmly, "if we were at sea, you'd be my first mate. You would write a note and stick it in that empty pop bottle of yours. Then you'd throw it out to sea. Bingo! It would bob around until it found someone to read it."

Christopher smiled sheepishly. First mate, eh?

But as far as Jane was concerned, this kind of talk was a waste of time. "Unfortunately," she snapped, "a bottle can*not* walk around Miss Pursey's yard and find Ann."

Suddenly she jumped up. "But Mashed Potato can!" she cried. She stooped over and patted Ann's gray cat. "Who would ever notice a little gray thing like that going over a gray fence?"

"No one," Christopher admitted dryly. "So what? What do you expect Mashed Potato to do—explain the setup to Ann?"

"Of course not," Jane sighed. "But Mashed Potato can carry a note, can't she? You know how she follows Ann everywhere. Maybe she'll find Ann, and Ann will see the note tied around Mashed Potato's neck."

"Maybe," Christopher grunted. "Only trouble is Ann can't read. Is Mashed Potato supposed to read the note to her?"

38

"Oh, Christopher!" Mary said crossly. "Don't be so gloomy. We can work it out." Already Mary had her paper and pencil ready. "We'll draw our message. If we can just get Ann to come quietly to the fence, we can work something out from here."

"Mashed Potato will be like one of those St. Bernard dogs that rescue lost people in the Alps," Jane said, untying the blue ribbon from one of her braids.

"Only St. Bernards don't carry notes," Christopher observed. "They carry bottles."

Mary shot Christopher a scornful look and went on with the note she was working out. She had drawn a picture of five stick figures behind a fence. All five had their hands up to their mouths. Above each figure Mary had written SH SH SH. On the other side of the fence, she was filling up the paper with arrows pointing back to the fence and the children.

"There," Mary said as she held the note up for everyone to see. "Even a five-year-old should understand that she is supposed to follow the arrows and be quiet about it."

Jane took the note and tied it around Mashed Potato's neck with the blue hair ribbon. Timothy gave Mashed Potato a good start by holding her up to the fence as high as he could reach and waiting for her claws to get a firm hold.

Straight up the fence Mashed Potato went like a helicopter to the rescue. At the top she balanced, looked at both sides thoughtfully, and finally

39

dropped, scratching and scraping, to Miss Pursey's side of the fence.

"There she goes," Patrick announced at his knot-hole, and Mashed Potato disappeared across Miss Pursey's back yard.

There was nothing to do now but sit and wait. Christopher passed out a package of potato chips. Jane suggested telling riddles to make the time pass faster but no one felt like guessing answers. Every few minutes Patrick would jump up to look through the knothole, but each time he came back with the same story.

"Nothing," he grumbled. "All quiet."

Christopher ran home and came back with a box of chocolate chip cookies. Now the only sound was the crunching of cookies. On the other side of Miss Pursey's fence, it was as still as the inside of a closed drawer.

It was getting near suppertime. Patrick put his lips to the knothole. "Here, kitty, kitty," he called in what he thought was going to be a whisper but turned out to be a roar.

"Sh," Timothy scolded.

Mary tried. "Here, kitty."

When nothing at all happened, they had to admit that not only Ann was lost but Mashed Potato too.

Christopher didn't actually say, "I told you so," but he looked so glum he didn't need to. He sat hunched up on the ground, the empty cookie box in his lap. He had taken out the last cookie some time ago, just to make sure it wasn't wasted, but he hadn't felt like eating it. He just held it in his hand. He didn't even notice Creep-up until it was too late.

This time Creep-up needed only one sniff to tell him that here was a smell worth saving. And it took only a snap of his jaws to steal this smell right out of Christopher's hand. With the cookie in his mouth, Creep-up ran off to bury it under the fence.

"Hey, come back here," Christopher yelled.

But Creep-up didn't. He went right on digging.

Jane laughed. Creep-up's whole body was trembling with joy as he dug frantically. He was digging really deep, sending dirt flying by the pawful in all directions.

A clump of dirt smacked Jane square on the chin. She put up her hand to wipe it off. "Honestly, Creep-up," she complained, "I wish you'd be more careful." She glanced at Timothy, who was brushing dirt off his shirt.

The same idea hit them both at the same moment.

"Go to it, Creep-up," Jane cried excitedly.

"Atta boy," Timothy shouted.

And then to everyone's complete surprise, Jane and Timothy dropped down on their hands and knees to help Creep-up dig.

"Brother!" Christopher moaned. "You're not going to *help* a dog bury my cookie, are you?"

41

But by this time, the hole was deep enough so that they could all see what Jane and Timothy were up to. Timothy was lying flat on his stomach and trying to wriggle under the fence.

A bit more digging, then Timothy had crawled through and was gone. Patrick made a dive to follow but Jane blocked him.

"Only Timothy goes," she declared. "Otherwise there would be too much noise. *She* would catch on."

Reluctantly Patrick returned to his knothole—only to find Chirstopher there and Mary behind him. When Patrick's turn came up, there was nothing to see. Timothy too had disappeared.

"Everyone disappears," Patrick complained. "No one comes back." But secretly he didn't expect anyone back until he and Lickety guided them out of the sagebush or canyons or wherever they were lost. Maybe they were all being held by bandits. He *did* wish he could see.

But if Patrick had been able to follow Timothy's path, he would have been disappointed. Everything was quiet on Miss Pursey's side of the fence. There was no hint of danger, no sign of anything extraordinary.

Still Timothy was cautious and crawled on his hands and knees over the unexplored territory between the fence and the Raisin. It was a wide stretch of land and Timothy went slowly.

"Ann!" Timothy called as he reached the front of the house, but there was no Ann.

He crawled carefully across the front lawn still strewn with rice. He looked behind the bushes near the house. There were several places here that Ann might have used for playing house, but she wasn't in any of them.

Timothy rounded the Raisin on the far side and reached the back, farther than any of them had ever trespassed before. Then suddenly Timothy forgot all about Ann. He whistled softly.

There was the tree. In all the excitement about Ann, he had forgotten the tree. Now it stretched up above him—the grandest, the most glorious tree Timothy had ever seen. He moved over to it in a kind of trance. What a tree! It was more wonderful than anything they had imagined from their view at the knothole. Timothy could stand up under it and be in a world all his own. The leaves closed around him to the ground on all sides. Sunlight drifted down in yellow slivers and patches. And when he looked up, all he could see was branches—crisscrossing, twisting, forming steps and ladders, swings and crossbars. He tried to follow them to the top and find the sky. The tree was so thick, so high, so intertwined that he couldn't see even the slightest patch of blue beyond.

But he did see a little corner of red.

Timothy climbed several layers of branches and

looked up again. There was Ann in her red dress. Above her, Mashed Potato was lolling over a fat branch.

"Ann," Timothy whispered, "come down here this minute."

A tiny voice drifted down to him.

"No," it said.

"Right this instant," Timothy repeated a little louder.

"No."

Quickly Timothy made his way up the tree, hand over hand, branch after branch.

"Ann," he said as he reached her, "you must come home now. Come on down with me."

"Go away," Ann pouted. "I'm busy."

But at last she did come with Lisa clutched under one arm. Mashed Potato followed, still carrying her unopened note.

Timothy gave the tree a long, lingering look, and started off again through the grass on his hands and knees.

"I can't crawl," Ann said. "I have to walk. I have Lisa."

"You crawl," Timothy ordered in a voice so terrible, even though it was just a whisper, that Ann decided to do what he said. At least this time.

The trip back took longer. Ann limped along in the front, using only one arm, stopping every few

steps to shift Lisa. Mashed Potato came next. Last came Timothy, fussing and scolding.

Finally they reached the hole and could hear quiet little cheers from the other side of the fence. Timothy imagined all the eyes that were taking turns at the knothole. He raised his hand in greeting.

Then Timothy grabbed Mashed Potato and pushed her through the hole. Next, he pushed Ann —a little harder, perhaps, than was necessary. Then Timothy, himself, wiggled through the hole and was met by a circle of excited faces.

"You're safe!" Patrick cried in surprise, as if he had been doubtful up to the last minute.

Everyone thumped Timothy on the back and treated him like a returning hero. They wouldn't even let him help refill the hole. But once they had stamped the dirt down, they wanted the whole story.

"I saw the tree," Timothy reported dreamily. He tried to tell them about it but he kept stumbling over his words.

"I saw it, too," Ann interrupted. "I saw it first. I sat in it and looked in Miss Pursey's upstairs window."

"Could you see anything?" Mary asked. Everyone crowded close.

"Sure," Ann replied briefly. "The shade was up. I could see a lot."

"Tell us!" They danced up and down with impatience. "What did you see?"

Ann looked around at her friends. She looked straight at Timothy and a secret smile came over her face.

"No," she said.

Turning her back on the group, Ann went home. It was suppertime.

Chapter 3

A T SUPPER that night Ann's mother noticed that she was unusually quiet.

"Where have you been this afternoon, Ann?" she asked.

"Oh, around," Ann answered vaguely, leaning over to pat Mashed Potato.

"Anything new on Pudding Street?" her father smiled.

"Not exactly." Ann was pushing her peas around her plate to make a design. She didn't want to talk. One minute there was too much to tell and the next minute there didn't seem to be anything. What had she seen, after all?

Just Miss Pursey sitting alone in an upstairs room sewing. From her place in the tree, Ann could even see the color of the button Miss Pursey was sewing. It was a large red button with a white pattern, but it wasn't the button that had been interesting. What was queer was where Miss Pursey was sewing it.

The button was not going in a usual kind of button place at all. Miss Pursey was sewing it right in

the middle of a sheet that was already nearly covered with buttons. Not only that, but on every wall of the room hung button-covered sheets.

Buttons, buttons, buttons! The floor was strewn with them. Milk bottles full of buttons marched out from the corners of the room.

And Miss Pursey was smiling! It was plain to see that Miss Pursey loved her buttons. She looked just the way Timothy did when he pasted a new stamp in his collection.

That was it. Miss Pursey was a button collector. Ann didn't know if that was a very important discovery or not. But she did know that a secret can be a very useful thing to have, especially if you are the youngest on a street. Ann was going to keep her secret. No telling when it might come in handy.

As it turned out, it wasn't the easiest secret to keep during the next week. First Christopher offered Ann two lollypops and a pet toad in exchange for the secret. Then Mary offered her a ride on her new bike. Ann just shook her head and tried to look mysterious until Christopher finally exclaimed in disgust, "Aw, bet she doesn't know anything!"

After that they stopped teasing her for her secret. Even so, it almost spilled out by mistake.

Once when they were gathered around the knot-hole, Patrick reported that the chairs were gone from Miss Pursey's gate.

"Guess she wanted to sit down," Christopher

laughed. And then he added as if he had never thought of it before, "Wonder what Miss Pursey does in that house."

"Just looks at her b——" Ann began and then clapped her hand quickly over her mouth.

She had to watch herself all the time because Patrick was always running to the knothole and Timothy did nothing but talk about the tree.

Timothy couldn't get the tree out of his mind. He described it over and over. Even on the Fourth of July when there were other things to think about, Timothy's mind kept wandering to the tree. There would be a faraway look in his eyes and then Timothy would be off.

"You know, that tree is so big," he would say, "we could all play in it at the same time. *If* there were only some way we could get around Miss Pursey. We could even have separate rooms," he would say dreamily—"*if* . . ."

But one day that faraway look was surpised right out of Timothy's eyes by a long, yellow sports car with brightly colored stickers on its windows. Timothy and the others were sitting on the curb in front of the Raisin when the car pulled up so quickly it made them jump to get out of the way.

"Don't tell me Mr. Shift is driving a sports car," Christopher whispered, unable to imagine anyone else stopping at the Raisin.

But it wasn't Mr. Shift. It was a businesslike man

with a straw hat and a brief case, who must have been expected because the gate was unlocked. He hurried into the Raisin and was gone long enough so that they had a chance to examine the car and the stickers closely.

"Rome, Paris, London," Mary repeated with awe.

"Cairo, Hong Kong, Beirut," Timothy read from the other side of the car. "You know," he added, "this guy travels. Wonder what he wants with Old Stay-at-Home Pursey."

Christopher was studying a picture of an airplane pasted on the back window. "Going Someplace?" it asked in black letters across one of the wings. "See your agent at the Globe Travel Service."

"Huh," Christopher snorted. "As if *she* would go anyplace!"

But the man with the stickers was only the first of a string of strange callers at the Raisin in the next few days. The gate was left unlocked all the time now and unexpected people kept passing through it. Twice in one day delivery men with lumpy packages stopped Patrick to ask where Number 121 was. Each time Patrick tried to drag out his answer so that he would have time to look the packages over but, even so, he never got an inkling of what was in them.

Not only was the traffic at the Raisin unusual, but even between visitors there was activity. Sometimes great rumblings could be heard from inside the house. Patrick thought Miss Pursey was bowling. Ann said it sounded like blocks tumbling downstairs. Whatever was going on, it was so far out of the ordinary that they all agreed Miss Pursey must have changed.

"I wonder if she still says *no* as much as she used to," Mary said.

"Well, I'm going to find out," Patrick declared. He was tired of watching and listening and talking. Before anyone knew quite what he was up to, he had unhitched Lickety and was riding through the front gate.

"Patrick, come back here," Timothy called.

But Patrick didn't. He just leaned over to pat Lickety. *"Giddyap,"* he shouted, and he galloped his horse up the steps and rang the bell at the Raisin.

"What does he think he's doing?" Jane whispered as they all crowded close to the gate.

Miss Pursey opened the door two inches. Patrick swept off his wide-brimmed hat.

"Howdy, Ma'am," he grinned. "Me and some of my posse out here are on the lookout for a tree to borrow. Think you could spare us your tree out back till sundown?"

Miss Pursey looked at Patrick as if she smelled something disagreeable. She closed her eyes and mouth to slits.

"No," she snapped and slammed the door.

Patrick hesitated. He thought of ringing again

because he really hadn't finished what he wanted to say. But then he shrugged his shoulders, turned and rode Lickety slowly back to the gate. He spit smartly out of the corner of his mouth as he came up to the others.

"No change in the old lady," he pronounced, making a circular motion with his finger beside his head. "Plum loco, that's what she is."

"What did you expect?" Timothy snorted. "An invitation to lunch?" Leave it to Patrick, he thought, to gum up the works. Any small chance to have another look at the tree was surely shot now.

But Jane was not so sure. Patrick's experiment had started her thinking. Anyone ought to know better than to ask Miss Pursey a favor, but perhaps there might be a way to strike a bargain with her. Maybe they could sell her something in exchange for a half hour's use of the tree. Jane thought of the brightly colored pot holders Mary loved to make but she doubted if they would appeal to *her*. Maybe they could run an errand. If it were winter, they could shovel her walk, but of course, it wasn't winter. Jane was still turning over possibilities in her mind when along came the tinkle of their friend, Wallie, the ice-cream man.

Maybe Wallie would have some ideas. He usually did. The most remarkable thing about Wallie was that he was grown-up enough to have superior ideas but at the same time his ideas were not grown-up at

54

all. In the winter Wallie went to college, but in the summer he grew an old-fashioned handle-bar mustache, climbed behind the wheel of his ice-cream truck, and whenever he could, he was a part of Pudding Street Plans.

"Here I come—ready or not," Wallie sang out as he pulled the truck to a stop. "Two vanilla cones, two strawberry, a pineapple, and a chocolate, as usual." He began to dish out the familiar Pudding Street order while everyone found a favorite perch on the truck. Timothy and Christopher straddled the hood, Patrick and Mary sat on the running board, and Ann and Jane were on the front seat next to Wallie.

"Now," said Jane, when she saw that everyone was settled, "we need your help." She told Wallie all about the tree and how they wanted a climb. Then she explained the bargaining idea she had been thinking about.

"Do you think it would work?" she asked anxiously.

"Oh, I do!" Ann cried before Wallie had a chance to say anything.

Christopher licked his cone thoughtfully. This sounded like the beginning of a Plan.

The tips of Wallie's mustache turned up into a smile. "I think it's a capital idea," he declared, "and I want to be in on it."

"What do you think we could sell her?" Jane asked. "Ice-cream cones?"

"Oh no!" Wallie made a sour face. "Miss Pursey never eats anything but pickles."

Ann looked surprised. "How do you know?"

"Oh, I know the type." Wallie nodded, looking wise. "Pickles, prunes, and burnt toast. Nothing else."

"Do you think she'd *buy* burnt toast?" Ann asked, amazed. "I could burn some—easy."

"No-o. I expect she can burn her own." Wallie leaned his elbows on the steering wheel. "Maybe we shouldn't sell anything. Maybe we should think of another reason for going to her house."

"Once we had an exterminator come to our house." Patrick glowed with pleasure as he recalled that day. "He went all over the downstairs with a gun, killing ants."

"No ant would ever move in with Miss Pursey," Christopher declared. "It would know better."

"Besides, we don't care about getting into the house," Jane reminded them. "We want to get into the tree."

"Well," Wallie began slowly, almost as if he were talking to himself, "I think maybe we have something here." He started to grin. "It's not only houses that have to be exterminated, you know." Wallie's grin turned into a laugh.

"Do you think," he asked in a deep voice, "that

you could make me look very important? Importan
enough to be an inspector?"

They looked at him doubtfully.

"Take off your jacket," Christopher ordered.

Wallie promptly took off his white ice-cream
jacket. Patrick reached into his pocket, pulled out
his sheriff's badge and pinned it on one of Wallie's
red suspender straps. He nodded with approval.

"You ought to wear dark glasses," Mary suggested.
"People in disguise always do."

So Wallie put on his dark glasses. "Like this," he
explained, "a little low on the nose so no one will
think I'm just a movie star."

Timothy and Jane looked critically at Wallie.
"What kind of inspector are you going to be?" Timothy asked, not at all convinced.

"A tree inspector," Wallie announced with importance, tapping his badge. "On the lookout for
Japanese beetles."

Timothy and Jane giggled.

"Only not Japanese beetles," Jane begged.
"They're too common. Zanzibar beetles. They're
deadly poison."

"And we are to be your assistants," Timothy
grinned.

"Of course," Wallie agreed. "You are to be my
exterminators. This tree, I understand, is so large,
it requires six assistant exterminators who will re-
main outside the gate until the job is secured. Then

when I say in a loud voice, 'Bring the spray guns'—out you come. And up we'll go!"

"You do have spray guns around?" he added hopefully.

"I do!" Patrick cried. "I have three of them. I have lots of other equipment too." He ran off down the street in a cloud of importance.

"He'll come back with everything but the kitchen sink," Timothy predicted. "You wait and see."

"Well, while we're waiting, we ought to think," Jane suggested. She sounded very firm, as if she had already finished all the thinking that really needed to be done.

"We have to think about what Wallie is going to say." Jane turned to Wallie. "You know that you'll have to talk fast," she pointed out, "because Miss Pursey is very quick at slamming doors. How fast can you talk?"

"Very fast," Wallie said. To prove it, he recited "Peter-piper-picked-a-peck-of-pickled-peppers" without a single mistake.

"Good," Jane approved. "Talk that way as soon as the door opens."

"You mustn't waste time being polite, either," Christopher added.

"And you shouldn't ask any questions," Jane went on, "because that will give her a chance to say no. Just *tell* her and talk official. You know, as if you had government orders."

58

Wallie nodded his head solemnly and cleared his throat as if he were about to demonstrate how a tree inspector should talk. But just then Patrick arrived.

"Look at all this equipment," Patrick shouted. He dumped an armload of supplies on the sidewalk at Wallie's feet.

"*Six* spray guns," he said and passed them around. "I went to Christopher's house and Jane's house too for their spray guns.

"Here's an old oxygen mask," he explained, "in case the spray is too bad. And the doctor's bag I got for Christmas. It says 'doctor' on one side but you can carry it so that won't show. And here's my policeman's hat and it doesn't even say 'policeman.' "

Wallie put the policeman's hat on the back of his head.

"Well, I'm all set," he grinned.

He took the oxygen mask in one hand, the inspector's kit in the other, and with his dark glasses trembling on his nose and the silver badge blazing over his heart, Wallie walked up to the Raisin.

Armed with spray guns, Wallie's assistants waited breathlessly outside the gate while he rang the bell.

For a while nothing happened. The door remained flat shut. At last Miss Pursey opened it part way and Wallie began to rattle off a volley of words. "I-am-the-local-tree-inspector," he said. "I-am-inspecting-the-trees-of-the-neighborhood-for-Jap— I-

59

mean-for-Zanzibar-beetles. I-was-informed-you-have·
a-large-tree-behind-your-house. I-must-inspect-it-im·
mediately."

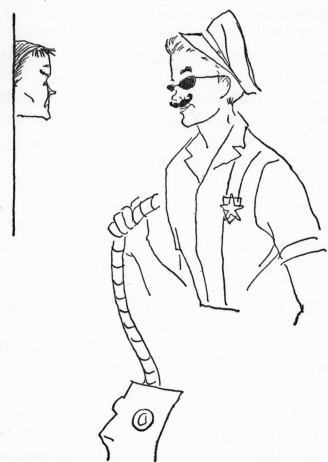

Wallie's voice was so gruff and clipped that back
at the gate the girls had to stuff handkerchiefs in
their mouths to keep from laughing and the boys
had to pound each other on the back.

60

But Miss Pursey did not seem impressed.

"Zanzibar beetles?" she grunted. "Hm. Never heard of them."

"Never heard of a Zanzibar beetle?" echoed Wallie in a shocked voice. "My dear lady, a Zanzibar beetle is deadly poison. Deadly." He shivered at the very thought. "Now," he continued, "I'll make my inspection, if I may."

"*If* you may, is correct," repeated Miss Pursey slowly and meaningfully. And bang! She slammed the door shut.

Out at the gate, everyone gasped. How did she dare? For all she knew, Wallie might have been a real inspector. He looked official enough.

"If there aren't any beetles there now," Christopher muttered angrily, "there will be before I'm through."

The door at the Raisin opened again. This time it was opened just a crack, and Wallie, who had already started to leave, wheeled around to see Miss Pursey's nose sticking through it.

"And you may *not*." Each word thundered out like a pistol shot from behind the crack in the door. This time the slam of the door was followed by a little click of the lock.

Wallie shook himself as if a pail of cold water had been thrown on him. Then he turned briskly and walked back to the gate, blowing huffily through his mustache with every step. He unpinned the sheriff's badge and returned it to Patrick.

"You kids better get yourselves a monkey bar to climb," he said. "Forget the tree. You'll never get far with Miss Pursey. She's a tough customer, that one."

Wallie went back to the truck, trailed by six pairs of dragging feet. He took off his dark glasses and policeman's hat, and slipped into his ice-cream jacket.

No one said a word. They dropped silently to the curbstone. Christopher turned to throw an angry glare in the direction of the Raisin. The air was thick with grumpiness and disappointment. Only Ann seemed to be looking more thoughtful than cross.

"Shucks," Wallie finally exploded. *"She* can't spoil a summer afternoon! Let's have some more ice cream!"

He went to the side of the truck and started to dish out ice cream. "This time it's for free!" he announced.

Christopher's scowl changed quickly to a smile and even Timothy looked as if he felt better. Ann jumped up as if she meant to be first in line, but instead she took off in the other direction, running down Pudding Street just as fast as her short legs would carry her.

"None for me!" she called over her shoulder.

Christopher looked startled. "She must be sick," he said.

"Maybe she didn't hear right," Jane suggested.

But then a moment later, just as unexpectedly, Ann was running back, smiling and shaking a round tin box.

"What have you got, Ann?" Jane called.

"Buttons," Ann shouted happily, but instead of coming to the ice-cream truck, she was *running up to the Raisin!* And she was ringing the bell.

Silly Ann! Jane smiled at her foolishness and they all held their ears against the awful NO they knew would explode from the Raisin, now that Miss Pursey had come to the door. Wallie started to dish out Ann's chocolate cone, but then he stopped.

Miss Pursey was smiling and Ann was going right into the Raisin. The door closed quietly behind her.

Five minutes later the door opened again.

"O.K., everyone," Ann called. "We can have the tree for two hours."

Chapter 4

WITH a whoop they sprang into action.

"Come on, Wallie, you too," Timothy called.

Wallie looked down at the dripping ice-cream ladle in his hand. He really should be going on with his route. He had taken enough time off already. Still, he would like to see that tree.

"Wallie!" That was Ann's voice from behind the Raisin.

Wallie tossed the ice-cream ladle into the truck and ran. Ann met him at the back of the house.

"There's my tree," she announced proudly, pointing.

Wallie took one look, then whistled—just as Timothy had done when he had first seen the tree. It was a long whistle that began high and swooped down to a slow landing. It expressed exactly what everyone was feeling.

Patrick tiptoed out from under the tree. *"Man!"* he exclaimed softly. *"Man, oh, Man!"*

Timothy couldn't find anything to say. His eyes were alight as he dug his hands deep into his pockets. The only word he could think of was—wonderful.

The tree was even more wonderful than he remembered.

"It's like a castle," Mary whispered, "with mazes and tunnels and circular stairways."

Jane turned and hugged Ann. "How did you do it?" she asked. "How did you ever manage?"

Ann glowed with pleasure. She had been right, after all. Her secret had been an important secret and she had known just when to use it.

"Follow me," she said. And Ann went up into the tree, hand over hand, climbing and crawling to the branch that almost brushed the upstairs window. A quick glance showed her the shade was up and she flung out her arm to point to the window.

"There," she said triumphantly, "that's how I knew."

Ann waited to see the surprise on the faces of the others as they looked into the Button Room. But they didn't look surprised. Their faces were blank. Ann turned around to see what was the matter.

And there was not a button in sight. The room was bare.

"But they were there! Thousands of them," she exclaimed. "They were sewn on sheets and hanging on the wall. They were all over the floor." Ann's story poured out. "And when I showed her that old box of buttons," she concluded, "she was going to pay me a dollar but I told her she couldn't have the buttons unless we could use the tree."

65

"How do you like that!" Christopher marveled.

"That was smart," Timothy approved.

"That was more than smart," Jane declared firmly. "It was colossal."

"Oh, I don't know," Ann protested, secretly agreeing with all that was being said. Everyone was looking at her and smiling. It was a lovely feeling, but then Patrick had to spoil it.

"Hey," he reminded them, "we don't have all day, you know. Let's climb." He hurled himself down the tree, shooting and spying, while the others set out to explore.

The first thing they discovered was that they could all be in different parts of the tree at the same time and still there was room left over.

"Can't see me!" Patrick challenged from a leafy hide-out, but no one wanted to see him. Mary had just found a robin's nest. Christopher had come upon a squirrel hole and was exclaiming over its size. He cleared out a handful of leaves and grinned. "Bet I could fit three pop bottles in here at once," he said.

"And a tray of ice cubes," Wallie added from a nearby branch where he was hanging by his knees.

And all the time Timothy was lovingly going over the tree inch by inch. "Look at this dandy spot for a tree house," he called. And a few minutes later, "Wouldn't take long to put up a platform here." He tested the branches all the way up and found them still strong enough at the top to hold him easily. He thrust his head up through the leaves and shadows into the sunlight. "If I could build in this tree," he thought, "I would build right here."

He took a deep breath, half expecting the air to smell different, and it seemed to him that it did. At least it was farther away from the trail of burned caps that followed Patrick as he galloped around the lower branches of the tree.

Timothy couldn't get enough of looking. All afternoon, even when the others invented a game of tree tag, Timothy stayed at the top, just looking. Pudding Street and the everyday world seemed small and unreal and far away. From where he was standing, Timothy could almost have punched a hole in a cloud, if one had been handy. He felt like Jack in the Beanstalk, at home with giants and winds and birds and anything else he might find in the sky.

"Hi, Crow!" he called to a black shape wheeling above him and he wasn't at all surprised to see the crow dip his wings in return.

This must be how it is in the lookout of a ship, Timothy thought, with the sea below you and your head in the sky. Only at sea the sounds would be different. He would be hearing the splash of water, the roll of waves, instead of . . . What was he hearing? For the first time Timothy became aware that he was hearing a great many sounds that were not at all usual around the Raisin. Of course the tree itself was noisy, but this wasn't what attracted Timothy's attention. No, it was the door-slamming that he noticed. There seemed to be a constant banging of doors followed by bumpy noises and strange voices.

Timothy was about to go down and investigate when over and above all the other noises came the very definite sound of a bell ringing. It started inside the Raisin and then grew louder and sharper as it moved outside and came toward the tree.

Timothy dropped quickly from branch to branch until he came to the ground. *Oh, no,* he thought as he saw Miss Pursey standing beside the tree, shaking a bell and glowering at her watch.

"Out!" she ordered. Miss Pursey bit off the word

as if she were glad to be rid of it. "Just like she'll be glad to be rid of us," Timothy thought. Then he noticed that Miss Pursey was wearing a shiny black hat. Not only that, she was carrying a suitcase.

Timothy gave a quick call up the tree to tell everyone that time was up and then he ran past Miss Pursey to the front of the Raisin. He stopped short beside a large pile of suitcases blocking the front path.

"Holy Mackerel!" Timothy exclaimed. There on the street was a moving van with two men loading it with an assortment of furniture that had been stacked on the sidewalk. And there was Mr. Shift trotting back and forth to his black car with suitcases and packages. Perspiration was pouring down his face and Mr. Shift was looking about as unhappy as a man can. As he approached for another load, Timothy cleared his throat and tried to sound casual.

"What's going on?" he asked.

Mr. Shift shot him a murderous look. "Going away," he answered briefly. He picked up a large cardboard carton and set off toward the car.

All at once Timothy understood. The delivery trucks, the strange cars, the lumpy packages—now they made sense. The rumbling noise must have been furniture being moved; the buttons had, of course, been packed away. Even Mr. Shift's strange remark the day of the christening had some point to it now—"Pity they couldn't have waited," he had said. All of it fitted together.

Timothy could hardly wait to share the news with the others, but when he looked behind him and saw them coming, he could tell that they already knew. Wallie and Christopher were sending him signals of joy behind Miss Pursey's back. Jane and Mary were trying to hush Patrick and keep him from prancing so much. Ann was aglow.

Timothy waited until Miss Pursey drew up beside him.

"Are you going far, Miss Pursey?" he asked hurriedly, trying not to sound too hopeful.

Miss Pursey turned and looked straight at Wallie. "Zanzibar," she replied.

Wallie swallowed hard. "Looking for beetles?" he asked weakly.

"No. Buttons." Miss Pursey snapped her mouth shut as if those two words were all she could spare. She raised her arm, pointed to the gate, and stood tapping her foot until everyone was out on the sidewalk. Then without a backward glance, Miss Pursey swept into Mr. Shift's car and settled herself in the front seat. She closed her eyes as if the sight of Pudding Street were painful to her.

She didn't open her eyes even when Mr. Shift came up with more bundles to load into the car. She just turned her head in his direction and spoke clearly enough to be heard on the sidewalk.

70

"You're slow," she said in icy tones. "Slow and clumsy."

Timothy looked at Mr. Shift's wilted face and stooped shoulders. The poor guy! Timothy was surprised to find himself feeling sorry for Mr. Shift, of all people.

"Here, I'll help," Timothy offered, and he picked up one of the bags and carried it to the car. Once everything was packed away, Timothy rejoined the group on the sidewalk to wait for the final take-off.

But there were all kinds of delays. Mr. Shift had to sign a paper before the moving van could leave. He had to go into the house and make sure all the shades were down. He had to write a note to leave for the milkman. As soon as he finished one job, Miss Pursey would think of another and call him to the car. And all the time Mr. Shift walked more and more slowly, muttering to himself, "Buttons! Around the world for buttons!"

At last it seemed to be time to lock up. Mr. Shift went to the cellar door and locked it. He locked the side door.

"Just so he doesn't lock the gate," Timothy murmured anxiously. "Oh, I hope he doesn't lock the gate."

Mr. Shift locked the front door. He tried all the downstairs windows. And then he started down the path to the gate.

"This is it," Christopher announced in a voice of doom. Everyone crossed his fingers.

"Oh, let him forget! Please, let him forget," Jane whispered tensely to herself. Patrick fingered the trigger of one of his guns nervously. Ann bit her nails and Christopher promised himself not to eat candy for a week *if only* Mr. Shift would forget the padlock on the gate.

Mr. Shift came to the gate. He hesitated a moment as if he were trying to remember something. Then he walked through the gate and onto the sidewalk.

He had forgotten! Oh, great day! Oh wonderful world! He had really forgotten. He was getting into the car and the gate was still open.

Just then Jane thought of a last question. She dashed to the car.

"Will you be coming back?" she asked Miss Pursey.

The car jerked to a start. Miss Pursey put her head to the window.

"Maybe," she said. "Maybe not." The car slammed away from the curb, up the street and out of sight.

"Maybe *not!*" Jane echoed, and as they all broke into cheers of victory, Timothy looked at his watch.

"Attention!" he shouted over the noise. "I want to announce, that at exactly 6:03 tonight, July 9th, the Raisin of Pudding Street was officially deserted."

73

Patrick opened his eyes wide. A deserted house! Things had been happening so fast, he hadn't had a chance to think of it quite like that before.

"Which means," Timothy went on, "that the grounds around the house and in particular the tree behind it are now unprotected, unattended—"

"And uninhabited," added Mary.

"And uninhabited," Timothy agreed. "I propose we take possession tomorrow morning at nine o'clock sharp."

Chapter 5

AT EIGHT-THIRTY the next morning Timothy was already waiting in front of the Raisin, slouched against the gate, and staring down Pudding Street. No one was in sight. In fact, the street was disgustingly quiet. There wasn't even a breeze to ruffle the morning. "Why didn't I say eight-thirty?" Timothy asked himself crossly and considered going home. But that wouldn't be any better; he'd still be waiting, only in a different place. And, of course, it wouldn't be fair to take possession of the tree alone. At least not until nine o'clock.

Timothy took out his compass and checked directions for a while. Then he found a piece of rope in a back pocket and practiced tying knots. After that, he took off his fresh clean sailor cap and turned it around in his hands to admire its whiteness. He looked at his watch. Eight forty-five. He would close his eyes and count to sixty, he decided, before he would let himself look down Pudding Street again.

But he was only as far as thirty when the first screen door slammed and a squeaking began at the far end of Pudding Street. Timothy didn't need to open his eyes to know that Ann was coming with her doll carriage.

"—thirty-one, thirty-two," Timothy went on as slowly as he could make himself. Maybe the others wouldn't slam their doors. Maybe when he reached sixty, he would be surprised.

But when Timothy looked, there was only Ann, a baby carriage, and three dolls. Ann started to turn in at the gate of the Raisin.

"Where do you think you're going?" Timothy demanded, jumping to his feet.

"To the tree, of course," Ann replied calmly. "Where else?"

"No, you don't," Timothy objected. "Not until everyone is here."

"I don't like to wait," Ann announced primly.

"You don't like to wait!" Timothy sputtered. *"I've* been waiting all morning."

Ann pouted. "Oh, all right," she said, and turned her attention to her dolls. "Timothy has so many *rules,"* she explained as she leaned over the carriage.

By that time doors were popping open up and down the street. Patrick stepped out onto his front porch, looked up at the spotless blue sky, glanced along the street, and then shot off his gun—as much as to say, "Let the day begin!" And he and Lickety set off for the Raisin at full gallop.

As soon as Timothy saw that everyone was on the way, he decided that it was fair to start for the tree.

"I claim top part for my crow's nest," he cried and raced through the gate.

"I discovered the squirrel hole. That part is mine," Christopher shouted, running after him with three pop bottles under his arm.

"Well, I'm going to have a section, too," Patrick

declared when they had all reached the tree. "But I don't know which part I want yet."

Everyone scrambled up the tree, but Patrick took his time.

"I want a branch that feels just like Lickety," he explained.

He straddled one branch, then another, but it wasn't easy. One branch would be too skinny, one would be too fat, and the next one might not be bouncy enough. At last Patrick came to one that felt just right between his knees. There was only one trouble with it; Ann was on the other end.

"Get off," she ordered. "I got here first."

Patrick bristled. "You don't talk that way to cowboys," he informed her.

"*I* do," Ann replied. "Besides you're sitting on Lisa's bed." Ann's face began to screw up, the way it always did before she started to scream.

"I'm sitting on Lickety," Patrick said. But the more he looked at Ann, the less the branch felt like Lickety.

"O.K., O.K.," he grumbled and backed off the branch.

Patrick looked up into the tree and at the very top he could see Timothy's sneakers. Scraps of song, like "over the ocean blue," drifted down through the branches. That meant that Timothy was all set. Patrick looked over toward the squirrel hole. The

78

necks of three bottles were poking out of it. So Christopher was settled too.

Then Patrick climbed across to where Mary was sitting on one branch with her notebooks spread out on a shelf-like section above.

"Not here!" Mary cried. "Don't settle near me."

"Why not?" Patrick demanded.

"Well, this is my desk," Mary explained, "where I am going to write poems. And a poet has to have a quiet place to work."

"So?" Patrick challenged.

"So you're not very quiet, Patrick, and you know it. Lickety would be bouncing around all the time and I'd never think of the right words." Mary licked the end of her pencil and went back to the poem she had started.

"Behind the Raisin is a tree—" she recited thoughtfully,

"Its branches spread both wide and free . . ."

"Yea," Patrick shouted crossly, "but it's not big enough for *me!*"

He climbed away and found himself suddenly backed up almost into Jane's lap.

"And I suppose this part is yours," Patrick exploded.

"No," Jane said. "I don't have a part. I'm still looking."

"Thank goodness," Patrick sighed. He threw his leg across the branch and smiled. It felt fine. There was even a little raised knob on the branch like the front part of a saddle. He tried bouncing and found that he could even plunge and rear.

"Hi-ho, Silver," he called. "This branch is mine."

And then, as he noticed Jane still prowling over the tree, he called to her. "What kind of a place do you want?"

"A good lookout."

"I know one," Patrick offered enthusiastically. "I was hiding in it yesterday and saw two Indians. Want me to show you?"

"No, thanks. I'm not looking for Indians," Jane replied. "I don't want to pretend *anything*. I just want to be where I can see real trouble when it comes."

"Well, this place—" Patrick started to explain, but he could see it was no use. Jane was trying out a spot over his head and she seemed satisfied. She wasn't even listening. Too bad, Patrick thought, because the place she'd chosen wasn't nearly so good as the leafy place he had in mind.

Still, she must have been able to see something, for already she was reporting activity.

"Christopher's mother just bought a pie from the bakery truck," she announced. "Mashed Potato is chasing a strange yellow cat off Pudding Street. And hey!" she ended with a shout. "Here comes Wallie! He's early!"

"I couldn't stay away," Wallie explained in the

tree a few minutes later. "Thought I'd let you show me around so I'll know where to deliver ice cream in the future."

They all conducted Wallie from one headquarters to another, ending up at the crow's nest, where Wallie and Timothy looked out over the rooftops.

"This is great!" Wallie smiled. "Even smells different."

"I think so too," Timothy said. "I just wish it were really ours. You know what I'd do? I'd build a deck right up here between these two branches."

"Why don't you?" Ann asked, crawling up between Timothy and Wallie.

"It wouldn't be legal."

Ann sniffed with impatience. "Oh, you and your silly rules!"

"That's right," Patrick agreed. "He's always making up rules. He thinks too much."

Timothy glanced at Patrick jiggling restlessly around on a branch below. "As for you," Timothy began, "you don't—"

"Come on, let's play," Patrick interrupted. "Let's play hide-and-seek."

Wallie put up two fingers. "Two games," he said. "I'll stay for two games."

Patrick scrambled away to hide in the leafy place he knew. He pulled the branches around him and over him until he was so invisible he pinched himself to make sure he was really there. Then instead

81

of looking toward the squirrel hole, which was home base, Patrick turned and looked out at Pudding Street. The view was good, just as he had known it was. Just as he had told Jane, but she wouldn't pay any attention.

Patrick smiled to himself. Wouldn't it be funny, he thought, if right now—at this very minute—something happened on Pudding Street. Suppose a masked bandit, a desperate one, galloped up on a black horse! Not even Jane was on the lookout. Only Patrick, himself.

But, try as he might, he couldn't see anything that looked the least like a black horse. The only thing coming down the street was an old black car. Patrick blinked and watched while it came nearer. Then he poked his head out of his hide-out.

"Hey!" he shouted. "Mr. Shift is here!"

Immediately everyone poured onto Patrick's side of the tree and looked with horror as Mr. Shift pulled up in front of the Raisin. Something certainly had happened, Patrick thought. But a bandit would have been better than Mr. Shift. What was he going to do? What if he had come to lock the gate?

But Mr. Shift didn't seem to be interested in the gate. Instead, he took a board, a hammer, and some nails out of the back seat of the car and walked over to the fence. Slowly and wearily, Mr. Shift nailed the board to the fence, returned to the car, and drove away. As soon as he was out of sight, everyone tum-

82

bled out of the tree. The next minute they were crowded around the board.

"What does it say?" Ann squealed. No one answered. There was only a long, hopeless sigh.

"What does it say?" Ann insisted and she grabbed Timothy's arm.

"For sale," Timothy read. Deliberately he took off his clean white sailor cap and slammed it on the ground. "How do you like that!" he said.

Ann started to cry. Patrick began waving his guns. "Over my dead body," he shouted. "Over my dead body."

"Aw, shut up," Christopher snapped.

Only Wallie did not seem disturbed. "Quit worrying," he advised. "No one's going to buy the Raisin. Who would want an old dark barn like that?"

"Someone like Miss Pursey would," Jane pointed out.

"But there couldn't be more than one Miss Pursey," Wallie reasoned, and Jane thought he was probably right. Still, it was better not to leave such things to chance.

"Listen," Jane said. "Some people don't care how a house *looks*. They figure they can fix it up. But maybe there are things about a house that can't be fixed up. Maybe there are other reasons why no one would want the Raisin."

"Like what?" Timothy sounded hopeless. "I can't think of any other reasons."

"Well, if there aren't any other reasons, we can just jolly well make some. We can do *something* to make sure no one will want the Raisin." Jane spoke with determination, even though at the moment she was not at all sure what they could do.

84

"I know." Patrick looked interested. "Maybe we could move a family of skunks into the basement." Jane flashed him a scornful glance.

"We could spread the news around that the house is haunted," Christopher said.

"I'd be glad to deliver that information on my regular route," Wallie said helpfully.

Still Jane shook her head. "Supposing there was a scientist who was looking for a house. He might love to buy a haunted one so he could find out scientific facts about ghosts."

"Yes, or a writer," Mary added, "who wanted to write a ghost story but didn't know any ghosts personally."

Timothy leaned against the fence and dusted off his sailor cap. He looked much happier.

"What we've got to do," he said, "is to change our tactics with each person that comes to look at the house. For instance, if a writer does come, the thing to do would be to—"

"Make a lot of noise so he can't think," Mary finished. "Patrick could take charge of that operation."

Patrick let out a couple of Indian yells to show that he was agreeable.

"And if a gardener came, we would let loose a gallon jug of Zanzibar beetles," Wallie suggested.

"That's the idea," Timothy grinned.

"One of us will have to be a spy," Jane said. "The spy will decide what kind of person is looking at the Raisin and let the rest know what tactics to use."

"You be the spy, Jane," Timothy suggested.

Jane had already decided that this would be by far the best idea, so she nodded quickly.

"I'll keep sharp lookout all the time we're playing. And when we're in the tree," she said, "I think maybe I better use Patrick's leafy place."

"I told you," Patrick crowed. He nudged Christopher. "I told her that was the best place."

Chapter 6

FOR several days there was nothing for a spy to see, and then when there was something to see, no one was around. Everybody on Pudding Street was at lunch, without an inkling of what was going

on until Christopher just happened to decide that he would eat his dessert on the front porch. Dessert today was a trickly, homemade, orange-ice pop. Christopher stood on the top step and leaned way over, trying to take a bite and at the same time lick around the edges, which were beginning to drool. His mouth was full of orange ice when he looked up and glanced across the street. There was Mr. Shift's car in front of the Raisin. Behind the car was a long brown station wagon.

For a moment Christopher stood rooted to the step, unable to decide which way to move. His ice pop dribbled over his hand and then fell off the stick with a little plop. But he didn't seem to notice. He just wiped his hand on his dungarees and set off down the street with the news. He stopped first at Timothy's and from there they went together, weaving back and forth, from house to house, gathering boys and girls and half-eaten sandwiches on the way.

"Of all the luck!" Jane exclaimed as they headed back under the hot noon sun to the Raisin. "No one around to see who got out of the station wagon! What kind of tactics can we use now?"

"Noise," Patrick suggested hopefully. "I bet noise would work. Let's try it."

But when they reached the Raisin, even Patrick could see that noise was not the answer this time. There was already plenty of noise at the Raisin. It seemed to be coming from behind the house rather than from inside, although the front door stood open and someone was raising the shades.

"We've got to investigate," Jane decided.

Stealthily, in single file, they went through the gate and up the path toward the Raisin. They were crouching low, circling the front steps of the house, when they heard a woman's voice from inside. It was a whining, worried voice.

"Wait a minute," Jane whispered. "Maybe we can get a clue."

But it was hard to tell what the voice said. It seemed to be darting anxiously from one part of the house to another. Only a phrase now and then could be caught as it drifted out the open doorway.

"I have so many of them—" the voice wailed. ". . . never know where they are . . . if there's any danger . . ."

The rest was lost or drowned out by the noise from the back which was getting louder all the time.

"Come on," Christopher hissed. "We're wasting time here."

They crawled around the side of the house. The noise was coming from the tree. *Their* tree!

It was swarming with children. Two little girls were rocking violently on the branches in the leafy lookout place, tearing off leaves by the handful and dropping them to the ground.

"Look at it snow," they screamed.

On a lower branch two boys were scratching and pulling each other's hair. "It's mine," one yelled. "I found it in that hole," the other screeched back while above them a third boy was waving a coke bottle wildly in the air.

Another boy was leaning against the trunk of the

tree and opening a pocketknife. "Let's carve our initials," he shouted.

And all the time Christopher's face was growing more and more purple. Patrick was blowing up and puffing out like a toad. "I'll show them," he finally blustered and started toward the tree.

But Jane pulled him back. "No," she said firmly, "not like that." She looked at the angry faces around her. "Follow me," she ordered and led the way around the side of the house, out the front gate, and to the empty lot.

They could all see that Jane had a plan, but at first they didn't want to listen. Each one had his own words to be exploded like a string of Chinese firecrackers before he could settle down. Twice Patrick and Christopher had to be stopped from going back and fighting it out with the intruders.

"It's the mother we have to worry about. Not the children," Jane pointed out.

"Well, I can't punch the mother in the jaw," Patrick grumbled, "but I can punch those kids."

"Will you listen?" Jane pleaded. "Think about the mother. Do you remember her voice?"

"It sounded mousey," Mary recalled.

Jane nodded her head. "Yes. She's the worrying kind. She can't keep track of her kids and she's always thinking about danger." Jane leaned forward and lowered her voice. "What that mother wants most is . . . safety."

Christopher stared at the ground. "The Raisin will be perfect for her," he admitted glumly. "Even the fence."

"Oh, Christopher," Jane cried impatiently, "don't you see *yet?* What we've got to do is to show that woman that Pudding Street is a very *unsafe* place to live."

Timothy straightened up and grinned.

"You bet it's unsafe," Patrick grunted, doubling his fist.

Jane sent Patrick a warning look. "We've got to hurry," she said. "I have a plan for what the girls can do. Timothy, you think of something scary for the boys to do. And *hurry.*"

Jane motioned to Mary and Ann and they raced off to Jane's house while the boys went to Timothy's.

In Jane's bedroom a few minutes later Mary was winding a roll of bandage around one leg. Jane and Ann were daubing Mary's other leg and one arm with some pink lotion that came out of a bottle.

"It's really hand cream," Jane explained. "My mother uses it, but it looks just like the calamine lotion I had to use once when I had poison ivy."

"Shall I just tell the woman I have poison ivy?" Mary asked. She didn't quite see how it was going to work out.

"Oh, I don't think you'll need to," Jane said and smiled as she pictured the scene. If this didn't scare

off a mother of a big family, she didn't know what would! She added a final splotch of lotion on Mary's forehead and then stepped back to look over the results of their work.

"You look terrific," Jane approved. "And remember—keep wiggling around and scratching your back as if you have lots more poison ivy where no one can see it."

"I want poison ivy, too," Ann declared.

Jane looked at Ann thoughtfully. She was wearing a pair of white shorts and matching halter top. There really was a lot of Ann's skin showing. It seemed too bad just to daub it the same way they had Mary's.

Then Jane giggled. "No, Ann, you're not going to have poison ivy. You're going to have *measles!*"

"Goody!" Ann cried. She'd always wanted measles. Everyone else on Pudding Street had had them and chicken pox, too. And she had never had anything. Except colds and they didn't count. You had to stay in bed with a cold and there wasn't even the fun of speckles.

"Say," she asked anxiously, "I won't have to stay in bed, will I?"

"Of course not, silly. You're going to the Raisin." Jane narrowed her eyes as she tried to picture the measles. "Do you think," she said, turning to Mary, "that crayon or water color would be better?"

"Water color," Mary said positively. "It's brighter."

While Ann squealed with delight, Mary and Jane dipped two fine-pointed brushes into a paintbox and proceeded to cover Ann with tiny red polka dots. It was wonderful fun, Ann thought, though a bit tickly when they painted the stomach part, between where the halter ended and the shorts began. She looked at herself in the mirror. Even her face was speckled like a strawberry and when she smiled, the speckles ran together in two circly lines.

"I've got measles! I've got measles," Ann sang out and started to do a little dance.

"Keep still," Mary scolded. "How can I work on your legs while you're doing that?"

Ann tried to hold still. She really meant to, but her right leg, all by itself, gave just a tiny kick before it settled down.

"Now look what you've done!" Mary exploded. The paint brush had jiggled and, instead of a dot, it had left a long, drooling red line down one leg.

Jane examined it. "Oh, well," she said, "maybe no one will notice. And there isn't time to do anything about it, anyway. We have got to hurry."

Jane stuffed the paintbox and brushes into her top dresser drawer. She'd put them away properly later. She reached into the back of the drawer and pulled out a rather fat brown paper bag.

"What's in that bag?" Ann asked.

Jane smiled mysteriously. "You'll see. It's my part of the plan. Let's go."

Jane went first, hesitating a moment at the top stair. It sounded as if her mother were on the front porch, sweeping.

"We'd better go out the back door," she whispered, "and cut across that way."

When they reached the empty lot, Jane paused to give final directions.

"The front door of the Raisin is open," she said. "We'll just walk right in—Ann first." Jane turned to Ann and looked at her hard so she would be sure to remember. "When you go in, don't look at the mother or Mr. Shift. Keep your eyes on the floor as if you were looking for something. Walk a little toward one corner, then turn around and say to Mary in a surprised way and pretty loud, 'Why, *I* don't see any white ants!' "

Mary looked a little doubtful. "Don't you think we ought to ring the doorbell first? It's not very polite just to walk in."

But Jane shook her head. "We are trying to *save* the Raisin," she pointed out sternly. "We have to make sure we get in." And Jane gave Ann a little shove to start them off. Mary followed Ann and behind her came Jane.

But when they walked through the gate they could see that their plan was not going to work out—at least not the way Jane had planned it. Ann stopped still. She didn't know what to do now. Mr. Shift, a woman, and a little boy about three years old were coming out of the Raisin. Mr. Shift stopped to lock the door while the woman and the boy waited on the step. The woman was as thin and worried-looking as her voice had sounded. She had a way of twitching her head quickly from side to side, as if she wished she had more than one pair of eyes.

"I think it's a lovely house," she said as she walked down the path with Mr. Shift. She fluttered her hands in the direction of the fence. "And I'm pleased it's so well protected."

Jane's heart sank. Were they too late, after all?

But Ann set her mouth stubbornly. She certainly wasn't going to have such beautiful measles for nothing! As the woman came near, Ann stepped right in her path and began to cough. It was a long, racking cough that went up and down the scale, from a frog's croak to a rooster's crow. Then Ann stopped and smiled sweetly.

"I can whoop, too," she announced proudly.

The woman looked as if she might faint. She pushed her little boy roughly behind her. "Why aren't you home?" she demanded.

"Oh, my mother doesn't mind," Ann replied and wondered if she should cough again.

But just then Jane stepped up. "Her measles is much better," she explained nervously. Really, Ann was going too far, she thought. She hadn't meant her to do all this talking. Still, the woman didn't seem suspicious. If anything, she looked only a little paler and very angry as she tried to back away.

But the little boy, who was peeking from behind his mother's skirts, didn't want to back away. He pointed at Ann's leg. "Look, Mommy," he said. "Look where her measles melted down her leg."

"Oh, *that!*" Ann glanced down at the streak the paint had made and laughed gaily. "That isn't measles. Only cats make marks like that. At least around here."

Jane looked at her in astonishment. Ann was certainly full of surprises. Still, she ought not to be allowed to go much further.

"Ann," Jane said, "I think it's time for your pill. You better go home."

Ann took one look at Jane and could see that she meant it. She leaned over and waved at the little boy still staring at her. "Good-by," she said. And Ann skipped off through the gate.

Mr. Shift, looking very mixed up, tried to take the woman by the arm and steer her away, but she didn't seem able to move. Her eyes had traveled as far as Mary and there they stopped.

"And *you* have poison ivy," she squeaked, and glared at Mr. Shift as if it were his fault. "It must be thick around here."

She looked down at the ground as if she expected to see poison ivy growing under her feet. She

97

clutched her little boy close and opened her mouth to say something further to Mr. Shift. But she never did say it. At that moment the boys on Pudding Street were ready with their plan of action. Creep-up came racing through the gate with Christopher tearing after him.

"Stop that dog!" Christopher cried. "Stop that dog before he bites."

Christopher and Creep-up disappeared behind the Raisin, but before Jane had time to see how the worried mother was taking this latest demonstration, Timothy charged through the gate. His hair was mussed up and he looked wildly around in all directions.

"Have you seen my pet copperhead?" he asked. He dashed from bush to bush, dropped on his knees to search the grass, and kept muttering that he had lost his favorite snake.

Afterward Jane could never quite remember in what order things happened then. She knew that once she had seen Patrick parading around on crutches. She remembered all the children from the tree streaming past her on the way to the station wagon. She remembered Mr. Shift shrugging his shoulders and muttering something about "What was the use?" After that he seemed to have disappeared in his car without saying anything more to anyone. But, most of all, Jane would never forget how the worried mother's head seemed to wobble dangerously on her shoulders, how she grabbed up her youngest child, and how, as she rushed to her car, her feet never seemed to touch the ground once.

"Whew!" Jane sighed, once the station wagon had driven off and they were gathered on the curb. "That was close."

"But successful," Timothy grinned.

Ann reappeared, holding a washcloth. Her face had changed from a speckled red to a smudged red and she was scrubbing at her stomach.

"Jane," she said, "what was in your brown paper bag?"

Jane looked down at the bag she was still holding in her hand. "I didn't need it, after all," she said. She put her hand into the bag and drew out a huge red firecracker. It was the kind that makes a double boom-bah noise.

"Left over from the Fourth," Jane explained. "I saved it."

"Oh, shoot it off now," Patrick begged.

But Jane shook her head. "No. We'll still save it. For something very special."

Chapter 7

FOR a while the boys and girls on Pudding Street were pretty cocky about the way they'd saved the Raisin and the tree. They walked in and out of the gate now as if they owned the place, and if the For Sale sign which still hung on the fence ever caught their eye, they paid it no attention.

"Pooh!" Patrick scoffed after the flight of the worried mother. "Why should we worry? We did it once, we can do it again."

Secretly Timothy didn't believe they would have to do it again. After that one try, Mr. Shift would surely never have the energy to come back. Timothy settled down in his crow's nest for the summer, his eyes fixed on the clouds rather than on Pudding Street.

Jane, too, stopped standing guard and seldom visited the leafy place any more.

The tree began to look as if they had moved in. Ann hung her dolls' clothes out to dry on all the sunny branches. Mary opened an art exhibit with crayoned pictures thumbtacked up the trunk. Patrick made a saddle out of a blanket and two old belts, and Christopher lined his squirrel hole with a sheet of tin foil.

Under Timothy's rules, no one, of course, was allowed to do any building or make any permanent improvements. Still, everyone felt very much at home and as if the summer couldn't possibly do anything but go on in the same pleasant way that it was going right now.

Even Wallie took it for granted that he would always be delivering ice cream to the tree. He was certainly not expecting any change on the afternoon when he noticed the sign. He was just about to dip into the bucket of chocolate ice cream when for some reason, which he could never remember later, he happened to look toward the fence. And he saw that the sign had been changed. The For Sale sign was gone. In its place hung a new sign. Even from where he was standing, Wallie could see what it said. On it was just one word.

SOLD

Wallie stood with the ladle in one hand and an empty cone in the other. When had the new sign been put up? he wondered. Had anyone else noticed it? All kinds of questions blew into his mind.

And then over the fence came the sound of Patrick's voice bumping up and down in a song.

"Whoopie ti yi yo,
Git along, little dogies. . . ."

Patrick sounded happy. Not at all as if he had heard any bad news. Slowly Wallie scooped out the chocolate ice cream and filled the cone. He would have to tell them, he decided. He filled the other five cones and walked back to the tree.

Jane was practicing tightrope walking on one of the lower branches when Wallie came around the corner of the Raisin. She jumped to the ground to help him with the cones.

"Hi," she said. "Will you teach me some acrobatic tricks this afternoon?"

Then Jane noticed Wallie's mustache. It was drooping badly. It didn't even turn up when Ann dropped from the tree and flung herself around Wallie's legs.

Jane tried to think of anything that had ever happened to make Wallie sad in the past.

"Wallie," she said, "have you had a fight with your girl?"

Wallie shook his head. By this time the others had gathered around for their cones and were looking with surprise at Wallie's long face.

Wallie blurted out the news. "The Raisin is sold,"

he said. "Come see for yourselves." And he strode back to the fence where the sign was hanging.

At first Patrick tried to make the letters S-O-L-D spell something different, but he couldn't. Then he wondered what good it would do to take the sign down, but that was silly too, he told himself.

"We can't change it, can we?" he asked at last.

"No," Jane admitted. "It's too late to change anything now."

Patrick automatically started to let out a roar of disappointment, but then he discovered that he didn't feel one bit like making a noise. He felt the way he had the time his birthday cake fell flat on the floor before the candles had been lit. It wasn't a time for doing anything; it was just a time for feeling.

"Well, that's that," Timothy said. What else was there to say? he asked himself. The summer was gone . . . over . . . ended. As for his crow's nest, he wouldn't even go up to it again. It didn't seem like his any more, now that somebody was going to move into the Raisin.

"Maybe no one will move in until fall," Wallie suggested hopefully as he climbed into his truck.

"And maybe they will come tomorrow," Jane declared when Wallie had gone. "I think we better move out of the tree. There won't be any fun in it now, anyway."

She turned to go to the tree and the others followed silently. Except for Timothy, who couldn't bear even to look at the tree now.

"We'll *never* have a tree like this again," Mary moaned as she took down her art exhibit. It was deliciously cool and shady in the tree. It was hard to believe they wouldn't be coming back. Never. Mary thought what a long word *never* was; there was no end to it. She didn't like to think of never going on and on, day after day, year after year, and so she switched her mind to the Raisin.

"I wonder who bought it," she said. They were all walking out to the sidewalk, their arms loaded. "Do you suppose it was the worried mother, after all?"

"What difference does it make?" Christopher mumbled bitterly. "Whoever it was, it's all over for us. And I wouldn't take two steps out of my way to find out who's going to live here." He raised his voice to a shout.

Ann walked out ahead of the others. There was no use her talking, she thought. They had all made up their minds that they would never climb the tree again. Well, *she* hadn't. She squeezed her armload of dolls tightly to her.

"You never can tell," she told them softly, and she made a little song of it. "Never can tell. Never, never, never can tell."

But when Ann reached the sidewalk, she stopped singing in the middle of a word. Then she smiled. She looked back over her shoulder and called to Christopher.

"You won't have to take two steps," she said. "Someone's moving in now. Mr. Shift and an orange moving van are here."

Mr. Shift climbed out of his car and stopped in front of Ann.

"Where's your measles?" he snapped.

"Gone—*long* ago, thank you," Ann replied sweetly.

Mr. Shift glared at the others. "I don't want any more trouble out of any of you," he growled. "Now go on—before the new owner gets here. Beat it." He waved his hand in the direction of the Pudding Street houses.

Jane thought of asking him who the new owner was, but she decided against it. Even from the back, as he went over to the moving van, Mr. Shift looked cross. Besides, Jane felt the way Christopher did— what difference did it make? So she started off down the street with the others, without a backward glance at the Raisin.

Only Ann lingered behind. "Never, never, never can tell," she went on singing while she watched the driver of the van open the back doors and begin to unload.

The first thing to come off the truck was a wire basket. It looked like a wastepaper basket but the things in it were certainly not meant to be thrown away. It was filled with candy bars and cookie boxes. Ann grinned.

"Never, never. . ." she began again but she

stopped as the driver carefully lifted from the back of the van an enormous object draped in a white dustcloth. As he set it down on the sidewalk, he flicked off the cloth. And there was the stuffed head of an elephant, the two white tusks pointing straight at Ann.

". . . *never can tell*," Ann finished with a shout and rushed down Pudding Street.

"Hey, come on back," she called. "There's an elephant head at the Raisin."

A moment later they were all sitting at the edge of the empty lot, watching the unloading.

"Aw—it won't make any difference who comes," Christopher still insisted, but then as a five-gallon jug marked SHARKS' TEETH appeared on the sidewalk, he added thoughtfully, "But it *is* going to be interesting to see."

"That worried mother would never have an elephant head or sharks' teeth." Timothy sounded more hopeful. But then a large tank of tropical fish was lowered to the sidewalk and carried into the house.

"She might have fish," Jane argued. "It's the only kind of pet she wouldn't be afraid of. Maybe each child owns one."

The next thing to come off the truck was a wooden Indian. Patrick looked interested. "Maybe a cowboy is coming," he said.

They kept guessing what kind of person could be

moving into the Raisin as they watched a tandem
bicycle come off the van—then a potted banana tree,
a harpoon, a hammock, a brass cowbell, a grandfather clock painted purple, three bearskin rugs, a
weather vane, a tent, a deck chair, and two large
wooden chests marked W.F.

"Well, *I* think that a lady named Wilhelmina

Featherweight is going to open a curiosity shop,"
Mary said.

"What's a curiosity shop?" Ann asked.

"A place where you sell curious things," Mary
told her.

But now Timothy was on his feet and walking
toward the van.

"It's not going to be a lady, at all," he cried.

Coming off the van and being lowered at his feet

was a rowboat. It was a big one—sturdy, freshly painted, and set on four small wheels. Timothy walked around it dreamily. Whoever is coming, it's going to be all right, he told himself. A harpoon, sharks' teeth, and now a rowboat.

Then he heard Mary talking to Jane. "Maybe she's going to plant the boat full of petunias and put it in the front yard," Mary said.

"It's not going to be a *she*," Timothy called back angrily. He didn't know why but he was sure of it. Yet a moment later he was as surprised as the others when a man drove up in a red car piled high with packages and duffel bags and with a tub of sunflowers sticking out of the trunk.

From one glance, Timothy could tell that this man was going to be worth knowing. He had a red bushy beard that went around his face like a ruffle and blue eyes that looked as if they couldn't stop laughing, no matter what they were told to do. When he stepped out of the car, Timothy could see that he was a big man, the kind who makes people want to stand up straight when they look at him.

Even Mr. Shift was straightening his shoulders now as he walked up to the man and handed him a large bunch of keys.

"Here you are," Mr. Shift said in the friendliest voice Timothy had ever heard him use. "Everything's unloaded and in the house. What shall I do with the rowboat?"

"Just leave it here," the man said. "I'll see about it later."

Mr. Shift nodded. "Hope you'll be happy here, Captain," he said. And he walked over to his black car and drove off.

Timothy's hand reached for the side of the rowboat as if he needed to steady himself. "Captain!" he squeaked in a voice so high he didn't recognize it as his own.

The man strode over to Timothy. "Captain Happy is the name," he said and smiled in such a way that his whole face seemed to be having a good time. "I see you are a man of the sea, yourself." He nodded at Timothy's sailor cap and held out his hand for Timothy to shake.

Timothy felt as if Christmas had arrived unexpectedly in July. A sea captain on Pudding Street!

"I'm Timothy," he said at last, but his voice was still a long way off.

"Glad to meet you, Timothy." The captain turned to the group of boys and girls who had come up behind Timothy. Ann took a step forward.

"I'm Ann," she announced, "and this is Lisa." She pointed out Lisa among all the dolls she was carrying.

Then, one by one, the other boys and girls introduced themselves to Captain Happy and shook his hand. When Captain Happy had met them all, he pushed his hands into his pockets and grinned.

"I knew it would be like this," he said. "I knew it would be fun to live in a place called Pudding Street. That's why I bought the house. Never even bothered to look at it." Again his face broke into merry crinkles, beginning at his nose and spreading out in circles just like a pool when a pebble is dropped into it.

"Now let's sit down and get acquainted." Captain Happy pointed at the rowboat and waited for them to climb in. But instead of sitting down, Captain Happy walked over to the door of the red car.

"First I'd like to have you meet my family," he said. He reached into the car and brought out a cage. Between the bars on one side of the cage, a twelve-inch tail curled. On the other side of the cage, a monkey was stretching out his arms as if he were trying to grab Captain Happy's pocket.

"This is Jib," Captain Happy laughed, "trying to sneak into my peanut pocket!" Captain Happy reached into the upper right-hand pocket of his jacket and pulled out a handful of peanuts. He gave Jib three of them and passed the rest around.

Then Captain Happy put his hand into his lower right-hand pocket and pulled out a fat white paper bag. "This is my gumdrop pocket," he explained. "Have some."

Christopher grinned. Timothy wasn't the only one to have something in common with this man, he thought.

When the gumdrops were gone, Captain Happy showed how the lower left-hand pocket was his licorice stick pocket and the upper left-hand one was his candy corn pocket. He was opening up the bag of candy corn when—*whoosh*—out of the car flew a red and green parrot.

"Thought that would do it," Captain Happy said. "She always wants her share of candy corn."

Mary smiled happily and hugged her knees. "Does she talk?" she asked.

Captain Happy shook his head. "No, never has said a word. Guess she's too shy."

And the parrot did act shy. She was hiding behind the captain's sleeve and ducking her head when anyone looked in her direction.

"She'll get acquainted," the captain reassured them. "Just don't ever call her Polly. Makes her madder than a trapped lobster. Her name is Porthole. Flew in an open porthole one day off the New Hebrides."

Mary nodded with approval.

"Have you any more family?" she said.

"No, that's all." Captain Happy smiled. "Guess that's why I'm so glad to see all of you. I like company."

Timothy took off his sailor cap and turned it over and over in his hands while in his mind he turned over the question he wanted to ask. Finally he shot it out. "What are you going to do with the boat?"

Captain Happy pulled the parrot away from his pocket and perched her on his shoulder. "Thought maybe sometime we'd figure out a way to float it," he answered. "I don't feel comfortable without a boat

handy. But for now—guess we can just park it in the yard. Want to help me roll it in?"

They all piled out of the boat and lined up on either side to push—except Ann, who sat down on the floor of the boat, her legs out straight in front of her, and said she wanted a ride.

Timothy took a front position and guided the boat down the sidewalk. For such a big boat, it moved easily, he thought—at least, on land. How would it seem in the water? He stole a glance at Captain Happy, who was pushing from the other side and across from Timothy. Did Captain Happy think there was any water on Pudding Street?

Then he remembered that Captain Happy had never seen the Raisin, and as they turned the boat through the gate, Timothy felt a cold prickly fear march up his spine. What did Captain Happy expect of the Raisin? Maybe he would be so disappointed he wouldn't even stay.

Timothy looked up at the gray house looming before him. It seemed almost to be wearing Miss Pursey's frown over its front door. Even its windows seemed to be squinting in disapproval. Timothy was afraid to look at Captain Happy. The captain wouldn't like the Raisin. Oh, it wasn't a house for a sea captain, at all.

Everyone must have been feeling pretty much the same as Timothy was. As they stopped rolling the boat, no one said a word. They just waited.

Captain Happy straightened up and looked quietly at the Raisin.

"Hm," he said after a while. "Best catch I've made in years." He turned to Timothy. "Can you imagine the luck? Might have landed a slick, new house with all the modern gadgets. Couldn't have lived in it. Nothing for me to do. Now, I like a house where I can make improvements."

He took a screw driver out of his hip pocket and strode up to the door of the Raisin. In less than a minute he had unscrewed the doorbell and dropped it into his pocket.

"Can't abide doorbells," he explained.

"But you *do* like the house?" Mary asked hesitatingly.

"Like it?" Captain Happy roared. "It's perfect! Can't wait to start improvements. If you come back tomorrow morning, we'll begin!"

"We'll be back," Jane promised enthusiastically and started toward the gate. She didn't really want to leave now, but she felt it wouldn't be polite to stay longer. Not the first day.

Patrick had no such feelings. "We don't have to go yet," he began, but he found he was mistaken. He did have to go. Jane had a firm grip on his gun belt and was pushing.

"See you in the morning," Jane called to Captain Happy.

Only Timothy stayed behind a moment longer. He couldn't quite bring himself to leave. He sat on the edge of the boat, swinging his legs.

"The Raisin can stand some improvements," Timothy agreed. Then, as he noticed Captain Happy's bewildered expression, he explained. "That's what we call this house—The Raisin of Pudding Street."

"The Raisin of Pudding Street!" Captain Happy repeated the name and a smile washed over his face like a wave.

Mary stopped at the gate and came back to the boat. Her feet squirmed around in her shoes, the way they always did when she felt happy. After all, she had thought of the name and now, when she heard Captain Happy say it, it sounded even better. But she had certainly been wrong in her guess about the new owner's name, she thought with a giggle. Wilhelmina Featherweight, indeed! Then suddenly Mary began to wonder.

"What is your real name, Captain Happy?" she asked.

Captain Happy smiled and jingled the doorbell in his pocket.

"Hap O'Leary," he answered. "But no one calls me that except for official purposes."

Mary looked puzzled. "Well, what does W.F. on those chests stand for?" she asked.

Captain Happy leaned against the house. He whistled thoughtfully as he looked up at the sky clouding over in the late afternoon.

"Well," he said. "So you noticed that. Hm."

When he didn't say anything more, Mary went on. "Do you have a cousin with the initials W.F.?"

Captain Happy shook his head. "No," he said. "Never heard of any."

He bent to unlock the front door. "Say," he called back over his shoulder, "hope you two will come with ideas for improvements tomorrow."

Chapter 8

THE next morning as they all walked up the street to the Raisin, Mary drew Timothy away from the others.

"I was reading a mystery book last night," she whispered. "It was about a pirate. Every port he went to, he changed his name. You don't think . . . do you . . . ?" Mary's eyes grew wide and she stumbled over her words. "You know," she added, "because of those W.F. chests?"

Mary watched Timothy's face and right away she was sorry she had brought up the subject. Timothy looked at her as if she had suggested that George Washington had told a lie or something.

"Don't be stupid," he snapped. "There aren't any pirates nowadays. W.F. is probably just an abbreviation for whatever is in the chests. Something personal, most likely. He doesn't need to tell you everything, you know."

Timothy stepped ahead impatiently but Mary caught up.

"Of course," she agreed. "Something personal." It was an interesting thought. "Let's see now. W.F. . . . W could be for Winter . . . Winter Flannels! That's personal. Sea captains probably do have to wear long flannel underwear in the winter, don't they, Timothy?"

Timothy set his mouth in a scornful line. "You should worry about winter flannels, when we haven't even found out about the tree yet."

They were almost at the Raisin. Mary put out her hand to hold Timothy back a minute.

"Don't you think he'll let us use the tree?" she asked. As soon as Mary had seen the captain get out of his car yesterday, she had decided that everything was going to be all right. She hadn't given the tree another thought.

"Sure, I *think* so," Timothy said. "But you don't know how a sea captain may feel about a tree until he tells you. Until he makes it, well—legal."

"Are you going to ask him?" Mary said. "How are you going to manage?"

Timothy shook his head. "I don't know," he admitted. "At least not yet."

But as they walked through the gate, they forgot their worries about the tree. Improvements had begun at the Raisin.

Jane and Christopher pointed excitedly at the front of the house where two ship's lifesavers hung between the upstairs and downstairs windows. Timothy grinned. It didn't take long to make the wrinkled old Raisin into a proper place for a sea captain to live in. Already the lifesavers gave the house a wide-awake look. And the door had been painted. It was a bright, shining red.

Timothy and Mary joined the others, who had gathered on the steps to inspect the door more closely. Ann put out one finger experimentally, but Jane pulled her back. "Don't touch that!" she cried. "It's wet paint." Jane tried to rub the red off Ann's finger, but Ann twisted away.

"How do we get in, then?" she asked. "If we can't touch the door, we can't knock. And Captain Happy has the bell in his pocket."

Then she noticed the gong. It hung at one side of the front door with a mallet dangling beside it.

Patrick saw it at the same time. "Oh, let me, let me!" he cried, and because it was clearly a Patrick thing to do, everyone stepped aside for him.

BONG BONG. The gong had a deep, underwater tone. Captain Happy stuck his head out of a downstairs window.

"You don't want to use a door," he called. "Doors are for company and animals. Go on out back."

The captain chuckled as he saw Christopher jerk his neck forward as if he hadn't heard right. "Go on," he cried. He pointed at Patrick who was al-

119

ready on the run. "Go on with Patrick. Out back. There's a better way."

At first they didn't notice anything unusual when they reached the back of the Raisin. Christopher looked at the ground to see if there was a new kind of basement entrance. Timothy glanced at the tree, not knowing where to look or what to look for.

Then all of a sudden a roaring noise shot out of a downstairs window and into the leaves at the foot of the tree. The noise was unmistakably Patrick. As they looked more closely, they saw a slide swooping out the far window and under the tree. It was a long, silver slide, half hidden by shadows and leaves and tall grass. At the bottom sat Patrick.

"It's wonderful!" he shouted. "Let me show you how it works." He jumped up and ran to another window where a rope ladder hung to the ground. Hand over hand, Patrick climbed the rope ladder and in a minute he was inside the Raisin. He re-appeared at the slide window and swooshed again to the bottom.

Ann was already halfway up the ladder. "I *like* Captain Happy," she announced, as she crawled in one window and out the other. She streaked to the bottom and then sighed happily. "I *love* Captain Happy," she said.

Everyone had several turns, and then, at last, out of breath, they stopped to look around the room they had been racing through. It was a large, dark, empty room with brown wallpaper and a moth-ball smell. Timothy had the creepy feeling Miss Pursey might walk in any minute, so when he heard a hammering noise in a room beyond, he followed it quickly.

And there was Captain Happy in his bare feet, dressed in a pair of paint-splattered white duck trousers, his back to Timothy. He was standing in front of the fireplace, pounding the elephant head to the wall above the mantelpiece. The trunk of the elephant curled up toward the ceiling, and on each of the tusks hung several doughnuts.

The feel of Miss Pursey had been wiped out of this room, anyway, Timothy thought. The windows were up and sunlight splashed wildly into corners and up walls. Porthole, the parrot, sat on a branch of the potted banana tree and Jib, the monkey, was rolling tennis balls across the floor. There were the smells of tobacco tins and clamshells in the room and the ringing sound of Captain Happy's voice as he sang,

> "Heave ho, my mates—
> The wind blows free—"

At the doorway the Pudding Street boys and girls listened, spellbound. When he had finished, Ann marched across the floor and pulled Captain Happy's trouser leg to get his attention.

"You aren't ever going to move from Pudding Street, are you?" she asked.

Captain Happy turned around and swung Ann high into the air.

"Never!" he said with a grin and set her back on the floor. "But once in a while," he added, "I'll be going away for short sea trips. Just to keep my hand in. But it won't be for long and I'll come back. Always," he promised.

He took a doughnut off an elephant tusk and tossed it to Christopher. Then he took a box of doughnuts from the mantelpiece and passed it around to the others.

"There's just one thing I'm worried about," Captain Happy said as he sat down on the floor and the others joined him. Jib jumped into his lap and Porthole flew over from the banana tree and perched on his shoulder. Captain Happy gave Jib a playful pat on the back.

"What am I going to do with Jib, here," he said, "when I go away on one of these sea trips? Know anyone who would care to feed a monkey now and then?"

"I would!" Ann cried eagerly.

"Good!" smiled Captain Happy. "Know of anyone who would wind a grandfather clock?"

"Me!" Patrick shouted.

Captain Happy took a notebook and pencil out of his pocket and wrote it all down.

wind clock .. Patrick
Feed Porthole -.. Jane
Water banana tree and sunflowers
·· Mary
Oil and ride Tandem..
Christopher and Jane
Dust Indian - Patrick
Brush 3 bearskin rugs - Christopher
Feed monkey named Ich. Ann
Feed tropical fish - Mary.

"And may I name them all too?" Mary asked.

"Aye, aye," Captain Happy answered and winked at Timothy. "As for you," he said, "can't let you take one of these jobs. Since you're the sailor of this outfit, I've something special you can do."

Timothy sat up straight.

"I have a short-wave radio set packed away," Captain Happy went on. "Want to teach you to use it when I'm at sea. I'll show you how you can tune in so I can talk to you."

Timothy gulped. "M-me?" he stammered. "Short wave—"

The captain nodded. He snapped his notebook shut and faced his audience.

124

"Now," he said, "there's the matter of payment. You are all doing so much for me. Can you think of anything, *anything at all*, I can do in return?"

Mary nudged Timothy but he didn't move. His eyes had a glazed look, as if he had walked away to do something exciting and had just left his body sitting there.

"Timothy," Mary whispered. "Don't think about the radio now. *Remember the tree.*"

At the mention of the tree, Timothy seemed to wake up. Of course. This was the time to find out about the tree.

Timothy stood up. Whatever he had to say always sounded more important when he was on his feet. "Well, sir," he began, "there's a tree out back—"

Christopher stared at Timothy in surprise. He had never heard Timothy call anyone "sir" before, but it sounded fine.

In fact, Timothy told the story of the tree and the Raisin so well that they all forgot for a moment that it was *their* tree and *them* he was talking about. Until at the end Timothy asked the important question, "May we use the tree this summer?"

And then and there Captain Happy hoisted up the widest smile they had ever seen on Pudding Street. "Of course!" he boomed. "Of course." He said it twice for good measure.

"I've seen this tree of yours," he went on. "Seems

to me it needs improvements too. Think you ought to do a little building in it."

Timothy stared, unbelieving. "You mean," he asked, "I can build my deck?"

"Sure. Build anything. All of you." Captain Happy made a sweeping motion with his hand. "I have plenty of lumber. I'll help. In fact," he added more slowly and thoughtfully, "I believe I have some equipment in those chests over there that might come in handy." He nodded toward the corner of the room behind the banana tree.

Mary looked toward the chests. She couldn't see any letters from where she was sitting, but she felt sure that these chests were the two W.F. chests.

"Are those—" she began, but Captain Happy interrupted before she could say any more.

"Yes," he said. "Those are the chests you were asking about. My Weak Fish chests."

"Weak Fish!" Mary exclaimed. It didn't make sense.

Captain Happy was smiling. "Guess I'll have to tell you the story about them. After you open them. Help yourself to anything you find."

But now that Captain Happy told them to open the chests, Mary suddenly felt shy and held back. It was Patrick who reached the chests first with the others crowding behind him. "Go ahead. Open it," Christopher ordered impatiently.

Patrick shrugged his shoulders. Fish—what did he want with fish? But he bent over and, without much hope, pulled up the lid.

The first thing he saw was a heavy white cloth spread right across the top of the chest.

"Looks like a tablecloth," he grunted. He was not interested in tablecloths.

Jane picked up the cloth. "Maybe it's a shower curtain," she guessed, but as she unfolded it Timothy could see it beginning to have a definite triangular shape.

"It's a small sail!" he announced joyfully and reached for it. "Look!" He held it up. "I'll put it on a mast and it won't be too big to go right on my deck."

Patrick didn't care what the white cloth turned out to be. He had caught sight of something in the chest now that the cloth was out. With trembling hands he reached into the chest.

"It's a *saddle*," he squeaked. He picked up a small saddle gently while everyone stopped to admire it. "What's a saddle doing—" he began. "Could *I* use it?"

"Aye." Captain Happy grinned. "Yours if you want it."

Jane was on her knees in front of the open chest. She had been pawing through a mass of pipe racks, toothbrush holders, dishcloths, and pillow slips.

"Here's something else for Timothy's department," she called as she pulled out a steering wheel.

"There's something for *my* department!" Ann cried and made a dive into the chest. When she came up, she had an Eskimo doll in her arm.

Christopher watched Mary open a brief case full of writing supplies and Jane discover a pair of slippers especially good for tightrope walking. Everyone else was having wonderful luck, Christopher noticed, but when *he* reached into the chest—what happened? All he could find were pincushions, ash trays, soap dishes, cases for eyeglasses. There didn't seem to be a single thing he wanted. He glanced at the book he was holding in his hand. *Farmers' Almanac, 1923.* He tossed it back into the chest.

Then he looked over at the second Weak Fish chest, still unopened. Maybe his luck would be better there. Quietly he pushed up the lid and saw that it was full of strange-shaped jars. Christopher chuckled. This was *his* department, all right. He lifted out a fat brown jar shaped like two bubbles blown together. On the front of it was written "Ginger Preserve." Christopher picked up the next one— Pacific Honey. Then quickly he lifted out jar after jar with strange and exciting labels—Pineapple Delight, Candied Foam, Jungle Jam, Ocean Smack. At last when he came upon a pink jar of delicious-looking Sugared Yum-Yum, he could stand it no longer.

Christopher unscrewed the lid and dipped in a finger.

No wonder it was called Yum-Yum. Christopher looked around. Luckily everyone was too busy to notice him scooping out the whole jar. He wouldn't even bother to pass it around to such busy people.

The treasures seemed to go on and on. Jane sat on the floor, holding her supply in her lap. "I'm ready for everything," she grinned. "I am going to be Vice-President in Charge of Emergencies." She held a pair of field glasses up to her eyes. "For sighting enemies," she explained. She picked up a barometer decorated around the edges with flying fish. "For storm warnings—dependable and accurate." Jane made her voice sound like an announcer of a television commercial. "And here," she went on, putting down the barometer, "is the answer to all your accident worries." She opened an elaborate leather first-aid kit and turned it around in a demonstrating kind of way so that everyone could see the three rows of bottles inside. "Snakebite, frostbite, spider poisoning, beriberi cured at no extra charge."

Jane glanced over at Christopher sitting in the middle of a large circle of half-opened jars. "Good also," she added pointedly, "for plain, old-fashioned stomach-ache."

Then with a nod in Timothy's direction, Jane went on, "Good for seasickness." She looked at Ann and Mary. "Housemaid's knee, writer's cramp, and —" But as Jane went around the room, she suddenly realized that Captain Happy was not there. She was about to ask if anyone knew where he had gone when his voice boomed through the window from outside.

"Ahoy there," he called.

Timothy was the first to reach the back window and see Captain Happy, standing under the tree. He had a hammer in each hand and was up to his knees in lumber.

"Ready to begin your improvements?" he called.

Timothy tipped his cap. "Aye aye, sir," he called and swooped down the slide.

Chapter 9

NEITHER Jane nor Patrick was interested in tree-building.

"When an emergency arises," Jane said, "I don't want to be bumping into shelves or tripping over rugs." So she hung her barometer on one nail, her first-aid kit on another, and slung the strap of the field glasses case around her neck.

As for Patrick—once his saddle was strapped on his branch, he was off across the plains, roping cattle and riding the range. He certainly was not going to mess up the West with planks and nails.

The others set to work with more elaborate plans. By the middle of the afternoon Timothy had half finished his deck and had figured out how he could put up a canvas roof that he could slide back and forth, depending on the weather.

"There's enough to do to keep me busy all summer," he thought happily.

Christopher had two shelves up in his section on which he was arranging his jars. He was considering making a counter if he could get Captain Happy to help. Right now Captain Happy was working on Mary's desk. He had spent almost all his time building for Mary and Ann, Christopher thought. He had

already put down boards for the floor of Ann's living room, and here she was—asking for more help.

"My doll beds won't fit," Ann complained. "I need more room."

Up in Mary's section, Captain Happy reached into his pocket for a handful of nails. "Tell you what," he called down to Ann. "We'll swing your dolls in hammocks. Won't take up any floor space."

Christopher frowned. "Well, I'm next," he declared firmly. He probably wouldn't get his counter started today at all. It was almost time for Wallie. And that reminded Christopher—he was hungry. He picked up the jar of Jungle Jam and was unscrewing the lid when he heard Wallie stop outside the Raisin.

Christopher smiled. Wallie didn't know anything about Captain Happy. Christopher screwed the lid back on the Jungle Jam and put it on the shelf.

"Sh," he warned everyone in the tree. "Let's surprise Wallie."

Christopher watched the side of the Raisin where Wallie would be coming. Wallie wasn't whistling, the way he usually did. Probably he was still feeling sorry about the Raisin's being sold.

Christopher winked at Timothy, who had climbed quietly down to join him. There was Wallie now. He was walking slowly, so busy watching the six cones he was carrying that he might not have noticed any changes on the front of the Raisin.

With his eyes still on the cones, Wallie called out, "Two vanilla, two strawberry, a pineapple, and a chocolate!"

Half hidden among the branches, Captain Happy

133

leaned forward. "Add one red raspberry!" he roared.

Wallie looked up so startled that everyone burst out laughing and dropped to the ground to tell him the news. Timothy introduced him to Captain Happy.

"Glad to have you aboard!" Captain Happy said heartily and Wallie, still in a daze, distributed the ice-cream cones.

"Glad to be aboard!" Wallie said happily.

Christopher took a bite of his cone. "You should have seen yourself!" He wanted to laugh but his mouth was too full.

"I bet!" Wallie agreed. "I'll get that raspberry cone now, Captain. Be right back."

This time when Wallie came around the corner of the Raisin, bringing Captain Happy's cone, he was whistling. He looked at the tree.

"Say!" he exclaimed, "where did all the furnishings come from?"

"From the Weak Fish chests," Mary explained. Then she remembered that Captain Happy never had told them why the chests were called Weak Fish. "You said you'd tell us," she reminded him.

Captain Happy took a long lick of raspberry ice cream. "Might as well do it right now." He sat down on the grass and the others dropped into a semicircle around him, their tongues on their ice cream, their eyes on Captain Happy.

"Well," he said, "I am the weak fish. Sometimes I am the weakest of weak fish. I can't say No."

Captain Happy shook his head sadly. "I've tried," he explained. "All over the world I've tried to say No, but I can't. If anyone wanted to sell me a cage of mosquitoes, I wouldn't say No. Not me! I might want to, but I wouldn't."

Ann's eyes widened with interest. "Did anyone ever try to sell you mosquitoes?" she asked.

Captain Happy smiled. "No, not mosquitoes, but everything else under the sun. At first I was so ashamed of the silly things I bought, I used to drop them into the sea when no one was looking. Like the gallon jug of elephant oil off the coast of Africa. But then I said to myself, 'Happy, old salt, you are not only being a weak fish, you are being a foolish one as well. You never know when that very jug of elephant oil might come in handy.' After that I bought those two chests. Then every time I was a weak fish and found myself with something silly or something I couldn't use right away, I just popped it out of sight into a chest." Captain Happy glanced into the tree. "Guess it was a lucky thing I did, too."

Timothy looked up to the top of the tree where he had temporarily tacked his sail. Only the tip of it showed, white in the sunlight. It looked like the wing of a bird, lighting among the leaves. "I'll say it was lucky!" he agreed fervently. Everything that had happened the last two days had been lucky, Timothy thought. Imagine—not only a sea captain, but a sea captain who couldn't say No!

"Some different from Miss Pursey!" Patrick exclaimed in admiration.

In the hubbub of excited chatter that broke out when Captain Happy finished his story, Ann nudged Mary.

"Do you think," she whispered, "that even if I asked Captain Happy if I could spend the night in my tree house—he'd say Yes?"

"Probably," Mary grinned, "but your mother wouldn't."

Ann nodded. That was the trouble with most grownups. They were always saying No. She looked adoringly at Captain Happy. "I want to hear you not say No," she said.

Captain Happy threw back his head and laughed. "Want a demonstration, eh?" he said. He turned to Wallie. "O.K., Wallie—try me out. I'll show you what a weak fish I am."

Wallie jumped to his feet. "Yes, sir," he said. He looked thoughtfully at Captain Happy, who was still holding the small end of the raspberry cone he had not quite finished. "Can I sell you a couple of raspberry cones?" Wallie asked, winking at Ann.

Captain Happy put his free hand on his stomach and pretended to groan. "Yes, yes you can. In fact," he grinned, "make it eight cones. We'll all have another."

As Wallie disappeared around the side of the house to fill the order, Ann smiled with satisfaction. "See?" she said. "He really can't."

"Well, that wasn't fair," Christopher objected. His face was a circle of smiles. "Who could say No to *that?*" Christopher followed Wallie to help him with the cones.

But almost immediately Christopher came racing back alone. It was clear that something more important even than cones was on his mind.

"Hey!" he said breathlessly. "Everybody get set for a real demonstration! There's a woman getting out of a car in front of the Raisin. She's got a bag. Maybe she's going to sell something." Christopher started to dash back to the sidewalk. "Save me a front seat," he called. "I want to see Captain Happy really turn weak fish."

A moment later Christopher and Wallie came back with the cones. No sooner had they handed them out than the gong rang.

"Out back!" Captain Happy called, getting to his feet.

Then around the side of the house loomed a figure so tremendous, so powerful, that it was hard to believe it was meant to be a person and a woman at that! She didn't look as if she had just happened to grow big but as if she had been built big, like a steam shovel, on purpose. In her hand she gripped a large, satchel-like black bag. She ground to a halt in front of Captain Happy, lowered her bag, then craned around to look at the boys and girls of Pudding Street, deep in raspberry ice cream.

"Aha!" she boomed and swiveled back to face Captain Happy. "Just as I thought! Raising a batch of kids and you don't know *that* much about it!"

She snapped a monstrous thumb and finger under Captain Happy's nose. Then before Captain Happy had a chance to explain that the children weren't his, the woman swung herself down and unzipped her bag.

Jane slid quietly along the ground far enough so that she could look into the bag. She didn't know what she expected, but certainly not brown jugs. There were three of them. One was marked CATTLE in long, uneven, gray letters that went up and down the jug like fishing worms. One was marked PIGS, and one was marked CHILDREN. The woman hoisted up the CHILDREN jug and turned a steely-eyed stare on Captain Happy.

"This is what you need," she bellowed. "Give them each three tablespoonfuls three times a day." She unscrewed the top and took it off.

Jane moved back quickly. Her hand shot to her nose to ward off the horrible smell that poured out of the bottle. It was worse than the most bitter medicine she had ever tasted, worse even than what happened when Christopher worked with his chemistry set. As Jane backed up, the smell seemed to follow

her. She pushed into the tight little huddle the others had made, as if by being close, they might all somehow have a better chance to survive the odor. Their faces screwed into horrified knots as they watched the woman lean down to take a strong sniff at the bottle, rock back on her heels, and shove her lips up into what was meant to be a smile. Patrick gagged noisily.

"Wonderful stuff," the woman bawled. "Will make their hair curl."

"Huh," Christopher snorted out of the side of his mouth, "has mine standing on end already."

The woman screwed the top on the bottle and thrust it under Captain Happy's nose.

"Five dollars," she roared. "Will you take it?"

Captain Happy moved back a step and looked at the ground. For a long minute, he seemed to study his feet with an unnatural interest. Then when he did look up, he looked at neither the woman nor the huddle of boys and girls. He just fixed his eyes on some distant point in space and slowly reached into his pocket.

"Yes," he said and handed the woman a five-dollar bill.

Timothy was the first to jump to his feet. "You don't want to do that!" he protested in a shocked voice as the woman took the money and marched off.

Captain Happy jerked his head to one side as if to shake off a bad dream. He stole a quick glance at the broad back of the Steam-shovel Woman as it retreated around the corner of the Raisin, and shuddered.

"How could *anyone*," he asked, "say No to a woman like that?"

"Well, I could," Patrick declared. He started off after the woman, but she had gone.

The boys and girls of Pudding Street exchanged worried looks. Captain Happy really couldn't say No, even when it was important. And now they realized this might be dangerous.

Jane picked up the offending jug gingerly between two fingers, and holding it at arm's length, with her head turned the other way, she walked over to the garbage can. In one swift movement she had the jug lowered safely into the can and the lid back on.

"Whew!" she puffed and walked back to Captain Happy, who seemed to have completely recovered his good spirits.

"It was worth five dollars," he was grinning, "to get rid of *that* woman!"

But Jane looked very severe. "Some time it might not be just five dollars," she pointed out. "It might be a lot more and you'd still say Yes."

"Pretty soon you might not have any money left," Patrick added. He was surprised to notice how much like his own father he sounded.

Captain Happy tapped some tobacco into the bowl of his pipe. He packed it down hard and reached into his pocket for a match. After several long puffs, he blew out a thin trail of smoke from behind his whiskers.

"I told you," he sighed. "I'd do anything to change, but it's no use. Unless *you* have an idea. You don't suppose there's a medicine that would cure me, do you?" He glanced uneasily at the garbage can.

"No." Jane folded her arms deliberately across her chest. "There's only one way."

Captain Happy blew a great balloon of smoke over his head. "How?"

"Practice," Jane replied shortly. "Practice and more practice. We'll give you lessons in saying No."

At first they all had different ideas of how to go about it. As Wallie started to leave, he offered to take Captain Happy around with him in the truck so that he could hear how other people said No, but Jane didn't approve. Christopher suggested that they take Captain Happy downtown to the candy store, turn him loose, and coach him from the side lines. But Jane dismissed that idea with a look of disgust.

"No," she decided, "we'll have practice sessions here and I'll coach. We'll try to sell Captain Happy something useless right now."

"I'll get something," Patrick offered quickly. "I have lots of useless things."

In a flash he was off. When he came back, he was carrying his father's brief case. He set it down at his feet, opened it slowly, and pulled out a battered, old cowboy hat that didn't fit him any more.

Patrick cleared his throat loudly. "Good hat for

riding," he said in a deep voice. "Keeps the sun out of your eyes. Twenty-five cents. Do you want it?"

Captain Happy grinned. "Well, now, let's see . . ." he began.

"No," Jane hissed in his ear. "Say No."

"No," Captain Happy repeated obediently.

"Say it louder," Jane ordered.

"*No,*" Captain Happy shouted and looked Patrick straight in the eye.

Everyone smiled with approval and Patrick reached into his brief case and brought out a large pink conch shell.

Timothy frowned. For a beginning test, this was going to be pretty hard on a sea captain, he thought. For years Timothy had wanted that conch shell for himself; it even smelled of the sea. He stepped up beside the captain to help coach.

"Fifteen dollars for this beautiful conch shell," Patrick cried. "Want it?" Surely not even Captain Happy could be tempted at that price.

Jane nudged Captain Happy, who was looking at his feet again.

"I don't think so," Captain Happy murmured.

"You mean—No," Jane reminded him firmly.

Captain Happy looked up. "No," he said.

"You can hear the ocean in it," Patrick went on, holding the shell to his ear.

Timothy gripped Captain Happy's arm. "Say— No, indeed," he whispered.

"No, indeed," Captain Happy said. Timothy relaxed his hold. It did seem to be coming more easily with practice.

"Say—No, thank you," he suggested.

"No, thank you," Captain Happy repeated louder. Then suddenly, all of his own accord, Captain Happy strode up to Patrick, stuck out his chin, and roared.

"No. No, thank you. No, indeed. *No, sir.*"

Everyone broke into wild clapping while Captain Happy bowed politely to the right and left and finally joined in the clapping, himself.

But later, in private, Jane was still worried. It wouldn't be safe, she said, to let Captain Happy go shopping alone for a while. And at least one of them ought to be at the Raisin as much as possible in case a No should be urgent.

Chapter 10

I T WAS, of course, no hardship to stay close to the Raisin. No one wanted to be far from either Captain Happy or the tree. Timothy's sail and steering wheel were permanently in place now, although his sliding roof had been forgotten for the moment. Timothy was busy with the short-wave radio set Captain Happy had delivered to the crow's nest. It sat in a weatherproof case, anchored to a small shelf, and poured forth a stream of messages from exciting places.

Some of the places had the most lovely-sounding names, Mary thought. She would sit at her desk with the new blue blotter and listen to the names drift down through the tree—Caracas, Amarillo, Bell Island. She whispered them over to herself. They were not only good to listen to, Mary decided; they felt good in your mouth as you said them.

But while Timothy and Mary might often be transported to strange and distant places, and Patrick spent more and more time on Lickety, the rest of the boys and girls of Pudding Street were concerned with the everyday business of the tree. Ann swept her living-room floor three or four times a day. Christopher gave his new counter another coat of red paint. And Jane traveled around the tree with her first-aid kit, examining everyone hopefully for injuries and reporting on the latest barometer readings.

Still, busy as they all were, they never failed to hear the gong at the front of the Raisin when it sounded. Usually it was Jane who answered the signal and ran to see who was at the door. If it was a salesman, she would stand by until Captain Happy had said the deciding Yes or No. It didn't take more than a nudge now to help him over the hurdle to a clear-cut, definite No.

But when Captain Happy was alone, it was different.

Rainy days when everyone stayed at home were the most dangerous. By the end of one day that had been especially stormy, Captain Happy had bought ten magazine subscriptions and two dozen candles. On another rainy day, Captain Happy went downtown and came back with an enormous box filled with hundreds of red and white plastic icicles for Christmas tree trimming. Timothy shook his head as he stored them away in a Weak Fish chest. Who could ever use that many icicles? Still, it might have been worse, he admitted. None of Captain Happy's weak fish purchases had been too serious. At least, not yet . . .

Timothy was thinking about this one morning at breakfast when he heard the heavy, grinding, chugging noise outside. He went to the window. A bulldozer was lumbering past and Timothy frowned. The bulldozer was going all the way down to the Raisin end of the street. Timothy sailed out of the house and after it, his mind racing as fast as his feet.

Oh no, he thought desperately. Captain Happy couldn't have done that. And yet, ever since the Steam-shovel Woman, something like this was just what Timothy had been afraid of. The Steam-shovel Woman could have sold Captain Happy anything . . . anything at all. Even a bulldozer.

Timothy turned in at the gate of the Raisin, still running so hard that he all but bumped into Captain Happy on his way out.

Timothy grabbed Captain Happy by the arm. "What's that bulldozer doing out there?" he panted.

"It's here, is it?" Captain Happy beamed. "Thought I heard it." He hurried on, tossing words over his shoulder as he went. "Don't know how we're going to get it into the yard," he said. "May have to knock the fence down. Better do it quickly, too. Can't rent a bulldozer and let it stand out by the curb." He walked over to talk to the driver.

Timothy leaned against the fence, weak with relief. The bulldozer had only been rented. Timothy scolded himself for having suspected anything else. "What are you going to do with it?" he called.

Captain Happy came back to Timothy. He took hold of the top of the fence, and shook it. "Won't be hard to knock down," he decided. "You and I can do it alone."

Then Captain Happy looked at Timothy as if he had just remembered he had been asked a question.

"Thought we'd dig a canal," he said. "To float our rowboat." Captain Happy stepped back and thrust his shoulder heavily against the fence. There was a ripping sound as several boards splintered and fell.

Timothy grinned. He hurled himself against the fence. He kicked at it; he tackled it. Oh, but it felt good to let all the excitement inside him loose against this fence. A canal, Timothy repeated. He flung himself against an upright board. To float a rowboat . . . He jumped on a pile of half-shattered sticks.

Just as the fence was down and the bulldozer backed out into the middle of the street, the other children came pounding up to the Raisin. Timothy explained what was going on, and they all stood back, with eyes shining, to watch the bulldozer bump up over the curb, onto the sidewalk, and crunch over the broken boards.

Patrick looked regretfully at the remains of the

fence. "And I didn't get one single swing at it!" he moaned.

"Hey, Bud," Joe, the bulldozer driver, called down. "Want to ride up with me?"

Patrick turned around but there wasn't anyone

behind him who could be Bud. No one was stepping forward to accept Joe's invitation. Patrick waited a minute to be sure. Then he spread his legs apart and jerked his thumb toward his chest. "You mean me?" he asked.

"Yea, you," Joe answered, his eyes twinkling.

Patrick spit out of the side of his mouth. "Don't mind if I do," he acknowledged and climbed up into the bulldozer.

They started digging a few feet from the sidewalk, ran straight down the length of the yard to the back —boring, gouging into the ground, backing up and plunging on again.

Joe glanced sidewise at Patrick bouncing up and down, holding onto the seat.

"Too rough for you?" he asked.

"Not for me," Patrick said but found he wasn't talking loud enough to be heard over the rumble of the bulldozer. "Not for me," he shouted happily.

All that day Patrick and Joe jerked up and down in the bulldozer, and by evening there was a deep, broad, ragged ditch in the ground. It was beginning to look as if it might really turn into a canal.

"Can we put the boat in it now?" Ann asked.

Captain Happy shook his head. "Not for a good many days. A truck and a crew of workmen are coming tomorrow to help out. Once the digging's done, we have to line her with cement."

Timothy noticed that now when Captain Happy

spoke of the canal, he said "her" instead of "it."
Timothy grinned. That made the canal seem much
more real, even if it was going to take a while to
finish it.

But Ann wasn't satisfied. "Can't we float the boat
tomorrow?"

"*Not tomorrow,*" Patrick replied in his bulldozer
voice and then had to lower it.

The next day Ann went straight to her tree house.
She wasn't going to be bothered standing around to
watch anything that took days and days. And once
the bulldozer had left, Patrick, too, found the canal
less interesting. But the others continued to watch
the work progress, dividing their time between the
tree and the canal.

Timothy and Christopher often picked up shovels
and helped with the digging, straightening the rough,
jagged edges the bulldozer had left, tossing dirt into
the waiting truck. It was fun to work along with the
men, to hear their jokes ring back and forth across
the canal. The men always referred to the canal as
the Erie and before long everyone was calling it that.

"How are you doing, Mike?" one of the men
would call.

"Halfway to Buffalo," Mike would answer. And
so the sidewalk end of the canal became known as
Albany and the other end as Buffalo.

Then one day the cement was poured.

151

"If she's dry tomorrow," Captain Happy said, "we'll fill her up and go."

The rest of that day no one could get enough of admiring the canal—gray and glistening with wet cement. What had so recently been just a wide, scraggly gully was now smooth and finished-looking.

"Neat as a bathtub," Christopher declared.

"Won't be much like a bathtub tomorrow," Timothy predicted proudly. "Not when the boat gets in."

The boat stood ready for launching at the Albany end of the canal. Already a flag was flying from its prow. Stakes for tying up the boat had been driven in at both Albany and Buffalo.

And all the time Timothy hovered protectingly near, first at one end of the canal, then at the other. If a leaf fluttered anywhere near, he was there to remove it before it could become embedded in the wet cement. If a dog or cat came within three feet of the canal, it was shooed off before it could even think of making a footprint.

At last it was evening and time to go home. Timothy followed the others out to Pudding Street with one final glance at the beautiful canal bed—rounded, smooth, and ready.

No one noticed that Patrick was still up in the tree. He was having saddle trouble again. The saddle kept slipping where it was belted around the branch. Patrick had blankets stuffed between the branch and the saddle, but still the branch wasn't quite as fat as the middle of a horse. Whenever Patrick galloped too hard or too fast, the blankets and saddle would slip and he would have to make a wild grab at the tree to keep from spinning completely around.

"Drat, drat, drat," Patrick muttered as he refolded the blanket and pushed it under the saddle. He rebuckled the saddle and gave it a sound smack on the seat. "There you are, Lickety," he said. "All ready for the morning."

Patrick climbed down from the tree and started home. As he passed the canal, he stopped for a moment. It looked rather bare, he thought—all that gray cement without a mark on it. And you couldn't tell what it was supposed to be. It really should have a sign somewhere—Erie Canal.

Patrick sat down on the ground to get a closer

look at the cement, to see if it was drying all right. It still looked wet. He put one finger on it lightly and when he pulled it away—there was the fingerprint as plain as day. It would be as easy as anything, he thought, to mark something right into the cement. That's what he'd do. Patrick smiled happily. He would write "Erie Canal" in big letters all the way down the side.

Patrick lay down flat on his stomach at the Buffalo end of the canal and worked toward Albany.

E—he wrote, big and bold, with his finger. Then he stopped. How did you spell Erie, anyway? Patrick remembered that his teacher always told him to break up words into syllables.

EAR—that was the first syllable. Patrick followed his E with Ar. The rest was easy—just add Y.

EARY

It looked fine. Canal was no problem. CAN and AL, and Patrick was done.

EARY CANAL

There was no doubt about it. It was a big improvement, he decided. Just wait until the others saw it!

The next morning Timothy was the first to reach the Raisin. As he walked through the front yard, he felt the sun beating down hot on his back. Timothy grinned. The cement would be dry. They could fill up the canal right away and have the boat launched before noon. Timothy tossed his sailor cap on the Albany stake and looked down into the canal bed.

At first he couldn't believe what he saw. Then he began to take it in. He wheeled angrily and stalked back into the street. As the others ran up, Timothy stood in the middle of Pudding Street and roared. *"Who did it? Just tell me who did it."*

Patrick had never seen Timothy so angry. His hands were clenched; he was breathing hard. Even his eyebrows seemed to bristle. Something terrible must have happened, Patrick thought. He wished he could do something to make Timothy feel better.

Maybe when Timothy saw the lettering on the canal, he would forget his troubles, whatever they were. But it wouldn't do to boast or talk loud when Timothy was feeling this way.

"Did you see the canal yet?" Patrick asked quietly.

"Did I see?" Timothy shouted. He turned and towered over Patrick, his neck forward, his eyes flashing. For a moment he didn't say anything more. Then he grabbed Patrick by the collar. When he spoke, it was in the most awful voice Patrick had ever heard Timothy use. His voice wasn't loud now. It was quiet but it came out sharp and clear even though Timothy's teeth were tight closed and his lips hardly moved.

"You did it," he said. "Why, you little—"

Patrick cowered. His mind was whirling around in foggy circles. In the midst of the fog he heard Captain Happy's voice from the front door of the Raisin.

"Hold on there, you two," Captain Happy shouted and strode into the street.

Timothy let go of Patrick's collar and turned to Captain Happy. "You haven't seen the canal yet, have you? Wait until you see it."

Marching angrily ahead, Timothy led Captain Happy and the children through the front yard of the Raisin and over to the canal.

"Oh, Patrick!" Mary cried when she saw the letters.

"You big dope," Christopher added.

Captain Happy patted Patrick on the shoulder and said it was all right. But, of course, Patrick knew now it wasn't all right, at all. It was far from all right.

"You might at least have spelled it correctly," Jane said accusingly.

"How do you spell it?" Patrick asked in a hollow voice.

"E-R-I-E."

Patrick pushed his lips together hard. Maybe that would stop the quivery feeling in his chin. He looked down at the canal. There were his letters— hard and dry, forever and ever—and misspelled.

"Well, maybe we can scratch something into the

cement ahead of the Eary to make it into another word," suggested Captain Happy.

"Smeary," Christopher scoffed. "That's what it better be. Smeary Canal."

Mary tried to think too, but there weren't any letters to make it right. Any letters that would fit in front of the "Eary" only made it sound worse—bleary, dreary, weary.

Patrick walked away from the canal and climbed up into the tree. It wasn't like a spelling test, he thought, where you could erase a mistake and write the word over. He wished he never had to see the canal again.

But every few minutes something made Patrick turn and look in that direction. First there was the gushing sound of water. Captain Happy was in Albany with one hose and Timothy was in Buffalo with another. Timothy seemed to be feeling all right now, Patrick noticed. He had his shoes and socks off and was laughing. Everyone seemed to be having a good time. Patrick turned his back again.

The next thing he knew Timothy was under the tree.

"Come on, Patrick," he was shouting. "We're all getting on our bathing suits while we fill the canal. Let's forget about that other business."

Captain Happy was there, too. "Come on," he coaxed.

But Patrick just sat hunched up on his saddle. He wouldn't come and he couldn't forget.

Later he could see them, still in their bathing suits, putting the hoses away. The canal was filled and they were lowering the boat into the water. Timothy was ready to take his place at the oars, but, instead, he stood on the Albany shore, cupped his hands to his mouth and called.

"I'm not going to sail until Patrick comes, too."

Patrick slid slowly out of the tree and walked over to Albany. After everyone else was in the boat, he slipped in too, squeezing himself into a little ball so he wouldn't take up much room.

They pushed off. Timothy rowed and everyone sang,

> Low bridge,
> Everybody down (and they ducked)—
> Low bridge,
> For we're comin' to a town.

Patrick didn't feel like singing, especially when they went past his letters. And there was no need to duck since he was already bent over.

After several round trips, the others all had a swim in the canal and then lay under the tree to dry off.

But Patrick just went on sitting on the end of the boat, tied up at the Albany dock. He felt hot and sticky in the bright sunlight, but he didn't move. He was facing the sidewalk, and now, with the fence down, he had a good view of Pudding Street. He saw the boy on the bicycle before he turned in at the Raisin. He watched the boy get off his bicycle, but before he could hit the gong, Patrick called to him.

"Western Union," the boy said as he walked up to the boat. "For Captain Hap O'Leary."

Patrick looked at the boy, standing there, so official with the yellow envelope in his hand. It must be fun to do something so important, Patrick thought. Suddenly he decided *he* wanted to deliver that envelope and he wanted to deliver it by boat.

"I'll take it to Captain Happy—I mean, Captain O'Leary," Patrick said, holding out his hand.

The boy looked doubtful. "You have to sign," he said.

"I'll sign," Patrick said firmly.

Still hesitant, the boy handed him a pencil and a slip of paper. Patrick signed his name and gave it back. He felt better than he had all day.

The Western Union boy, however, still did not give Patrick the yellow envelope. He looked up from the slip of paper.

"Your name's not O'Leary," he said. "You live here?"

"Um," Patrick grunted. Well, he *almost* did, and he hadn't really said yes. Then when the boy kept on standing there, Patrick became impatient. "See that

159

man lying over there under the tree? That's the captain. I'll take it right to him."

At last the Western Union boy handed Patrick the telegram. Patrick stuck it quickly into his pocket, untied the boat, and rowed to Buffalo so fast the waves slopped up over the banks. He threw the rope over the stake and strode over to Captain Happy.

"Western Union," Patrick announced, pulling the yellow envelope out of his pocket.

Captain Happy tore open the envelope. He looked at all the attentive faces around him and read the telegram aloud.

"Captain Hap O'Leary," he read, "to report to Steamer *Merryweather* for ten-day cruise, August 25."

"August twenty-fifth!" Jane gasped. "That's to-morrow!"

"Aye." Captain Happy rose heavily to his feet. "Sooner than I expected. Better get ready, hadn't I?"

They all jumped up to follow Captain Happy into the Raisin. Patrick stopped to pick up the telegram that had fallen to the ground.

"Captain Hap O'Leary," he read as he followed the others. There was something about that name that puzzled Patrick. Then suddenly he knew. Captain Happy's name was O'Leary. O apostrophe L and EARY.

Patrick's face broke into a ring of smiles. "Say,

Timothy," he called. "How about naming the canal the O'Leary Canal? We could scratch O apostrophe L in the cement easy."

Timothy grinned. He looked at Patrick in a respectful way, as if he were somebody important, like a Western Union boy.

"That's great," Timothy said. "Super."

Patrick swaggered along happily in the rear.

Chapter II

THE next morning they were standing on the curb in front of the Raisin when Captain Happy came out, a suitcase in each hand. It was the first time any of them had seen Captain Happy in full uniform.

"Isn't he beautiful?" Ann breathed, unable to take her eyes off the dazzling spectacle of Captain Happy a-shine with brass buttons.

Timothy held the door open while Captain Happy slid into his red convertible.

"I'll be talking to you," Captain Happy said, turning to Timothy. "Day after tomorrow. Try to contact me on the radio about sixteen hundred."

Timothy nodded. He'd explain to the others later that in navy talk, sixteen hundred meant four o'clock in the afternoon.

"After that, for the next few days, tune in on me twice daily—ten hundred and sixteen hundred." Captain Happy beamed at the boys and girls crowding around the door of the car, "Before you know it, I'll be back!"

Captain Happy started up the engine and amid an

162

uproar of good-bys drove off down Pudding Street.
No one moved until the last flash of red had disappeared around the corner. Even then Ann kept right
on waving. When at last she did drop her arm and
turn around, there were two fat tears brimming in
her eyes.

"I'm lonely," Ann said.

Christopher, too, had an empty feeling in the
bottom of his stomach, not like his usual empty feeling at all. Patrick shuffled around on the sidewalk.
"Isn't it quiet!" he commented uneasily.

Jane took one look at the despondent group,
turned briskly and started for the Raisin. "Time for
Porthole's breakfast," she announced over her shoulder.

Everyone sprang to attention. Their jobs were
waiting.

As she ran around to the back of the house to
climb up the rope ladder, Mary felt in the pocket of
her blue jeans. Yes, she had the chart she had made
last night. She hurried into the kitchen and in a
minute was tacking the chart up on the bulletin
board. No one had any excuse now, she thought, for
forgetting his job. She stepped back to admire the
chart.

WIND CLOCK*************PATRICK
FEED PORTHOLE*********JANE
WATER BANANA TREE****MARY

163

```
WATER SUNFLOWERS******MARY
DUST  INDIAN************PATRICK
RIDE TANDEM AND OIL IT*CHRISTOPHER
                    AND JANE
BRUSH BEAR RUGS*******CHRISTOPHER
FEED JIB*****************ANN
FEED TROPICAL FISH******MARY
OPERATE  RADIO*********TIMOTHY
```

It looked both official and artistic. Of course, Mary had to admit to herself, she didn't think anyone was going to need reminding.

She picked up the watering can to tend to the banana tree and sunflowers. She glanced over at Patrick, already vigorously dusting and polishing the wooden Indian. If a spot didn't look bright enough, he spit at it and went over it again. Mary could see that Patrick certainly wasn't going to need reminding. If anything, he would have to be kept from overdoing his work.

As the day went on, it was clear that Ann would need no reminding, either. The first time she fed Jib, the monkey apparently understood that she was his new mistress and decided he wasn't going to let her out of his sight.

"He likes me!" Ann cried with delight as Jib gulped down his breakfast and followed her out to the tree. "I think I better keep a peanut pocket like Captain Happy does."

164

But by afternoon Ann had discarded the peanuts.
She sat forlornly on the ground with Jib in her lap

and watched everyone else play a game of tree tag.
Halfheartedly she patted Jib's head.

"I'm glad you love me," she said, "but I do wish
you didn't love me quite so hard."

She sighed as Jib flung himself into a frenzy of chatter. Ann knew, of course, that he was trying to say that he couldn't help loving her, but she sighed again.

"I think you can help it," she argued. "I don't see why you can't sit quietly in the tree and let me play tag with the others."

But when Ann tried to put Jib in the tree, he flung his arms around her neck again and whimpered. How could you play tree tag with a monkey draped around your neck? In fact, how could you do anything, Ann wondered.

The next day was even worse. Ann wanted to play in her tree house. She hadn't given Lisa a bath for three days and she thought that maybe she could manage, even if Jib did sit in her lap. Ann got out her bathinette and filled it with water from the canal. With Mary's help she succeeded in getting it safely into the tree. Jib followed every step of the way, scolding and swinging on her skirt, but once Ann sat down, Jib settled down quietly enough in her lap.

Ann reached into the box where she kept Lisa's things and took out a towel and a clean dress. Then she reached up into a hammock and picked up Lisa. For a moment she was so busy unbuttoning Lisa's nightgown that she didn't notice Jib.

Mary on the branch above saw Jib crook his tail and narrow his eyes in anger.

"Watch out!" Mary cried. But it was too late. Jib had made a wild spring at Lisa and came away with a handful of golden hair.

"Stop it, Jib, stop it," Ann shrieked, pushing Lisa hurriedly back into her hammock. Right away Jib quieted down and curled up again in Ann's lap.

"Why, he's jealous!" Mary exclaimed. "Let's see if he does anything when I pick up Lisa." She stooped down and picked up Lisa, but Jib couldn't have cared less. He closed his eyes and snuggled deeper into Ann's lap.

"It's just you," Mary concluded and put Lisa back, reassuring Ann that Lisa had not really been hurt at all.

After that, Ann didn't dare play with her dolls. There just didn't seem to be anything to do. She moped around the back yard with Jib, wishing she had been given an easy job like feeding some silly fish or dusting an old wooden Indian.

She tried putting Jib in his cage but that didn't work either. He pretended to be sick. Then he held his breath. Everyone told Ann that Jib was just putting on an act, but she didn't dare take a chance. Jib was her responsibility.

But the next afternoon Ann really got mad.

"All right," she said to Jib, "if you're not going to let me play with my dolls, you'll have to be a doll."

Ann wheeled up her baby carriage, held Jib firmly

between her knees, and dressed him in her biggest baby doll dress. She tied a pink lace bonnet around his head and pushed his legs roughly into a pair of rubber panties. As a last touch she added a white wool sweater, set him in the carriage, and pulled a blue blanket over his feet.

"I don't care if you are hot," Ann declared crossly.

But Jib didn't seem hot. He only seemed happy. He settled back on his pillow, looking so sweet that Ann's heart softened. She patted him through the covers. After all, it was probably a good idea to dress Jib warmly. It was what Ann called an "off and on" day—cloudy one minute, sunny the next. It was best for a mother to be ready for all kinds of weather.

"You know what," she said gently, "I'm going to wheel you right up street."

Jib lay still and looked lovingly up at Ann. A moment later he started to make a soft cooing noise— something Ann had never heard him do before. He sounded like a real baby, she thought, and she beamed with pride.

"Look at me!" she called to Christopher and Jane as they rode past on the tandem.

The farther Ann went, the prouder she felt. "I am going to wheel Jib right to the Five and Ten," she decided, "and I'm going to buy him a rattle all his own." She felt in her pocket to make sure of her dime.

Ann was so pleased she skipped a couple of steps, then settled down to a more dignified walk, stopping often to adjust the hood of the carriage or fuss with Jib's covers, the way real mothers did. She passed Christopher and Jane, who were looking in the bakery window.

"Remember, Ann, don't cross any streets," Jane called loudly.

Ann jerked her shoulder impatiently. She didn't have to cross any streets to go to the Five and Ten. She wished Jane would mind her own business, anyway. Ann raised herself on her toes and tried a teetering kind of walk, as if she were wearing high heels. She glanced at herself in a store window and thought how grown-up she looked. She just hoped she wouldn't run into Jane again.

Ann turned into the Five and Ten and started toward the toy counter. The aisle was so narrow it wasn't easy to manage the carriage.

"Excuse me," Ann murmured to several pairs of legs blocking the aisle by the thread counter.

"Excuse me," she said again, but no one budged. Ann looked up and saw two women with long noses like Miss Pursey's, holding spools of thread up to the light.

"Oh, well . . ." Ann sighed and turned around and went down another aisle. She reached the toy counter with Jib still behaving so perfectly, she was sure no one suspected he wasn't a baby.

Ann put the brake on the carriage and turned to the counter. There was a lovely blue rattle with a teething ring on one end. Ann paid for it and handed it to Jib, who took it as calmly as if rattles were given to him every day in the week. He waved it gently and tried out the teething ring.

"Now that he's taken care of," Ann told herself in a motherly fashion, "I think I'll just look around a little, myself."

She looked at the jump ropes and the toy washing machines and the dish sets. She looked at the games and was going through the coloring books when she saw the doll. It wasn't a very big doll; it could fit into a pocket. But it had real golden hair and a blue satin skirt that twirled. Carefully Ann reached out her hand and picked it up.

Whoosh!

Jib shot out of the carriage and onto the counter like a skyrocket. He slapped the doll's face and pinched her arm. He jumped up and down on a box of dominoes. Before Ann could grab him, he had made a leap, his doll dress flying behind him, over to the . . . thread counter! He stooped and picked up as many spools of thread as he could hold in two hands and began to throw them wildly in all directions.

Just at that moment Christopher and Jane walked

into the Five and Ten. Behind them came the Chief
of Police. Jane looked first at the screaming custom-
ers, then at Jib—his bonnet askew, his dress torn.
And finally she looked at Ann standing by the toy

counter, crying and holding onto a small pocket-size doll.

"Ann," Jane cried, "drop that doll!"

In her fright Ann had forgotten the doll. Quickly she put it on the counter. Immediately (*immediately,* Jane emphasized later when she told the story) Jib straightened his bonnet, hopped back across the store and into his carriage, and pulled the blue blanket up to his chin.

Ann wiped her eyes with the back of her hand and decided to get out of the store as fast as she could. But there were those women, blocking her way again!

"Do something," the taller woman was screaming at the Chief of Police. "Do something to these, these . . . hooligans." She pointed at Ann, Jane, and Christopher. "Ought to be locked up," she said, "all of them."

The Chief of Police pushed his hat back on his head.

"Come with me," he said gruffly.

There was nothing else to do. Christopher, Jane, and Ann followed the Chief out of the store, feeling more and more like hooligans with every step they took. On the sidewalk, however, the Chief didn't turn in the direction of the police station as they had expected he would. In fact, he turned just the opposite way as if he were going toward Pudding Street.

He marched out in front of them, twirling his billy club and never once looking back over his shoulder.

He walked so fast, it was hard to keep up. Jane and Christopher thought riding the tandem while the Chief walked would seem disrespectful, so they pushed it awkwardly between them. Ann was so upset that she kept bumping into them with her carriage.

When they reached Pudding Street, the Chief turned. He led them past all their houses, past the empty lot, to the door of the Raisin. Then he swung around and faced them.

"Heard about you kids," he barked. "Known the captain since we were boys together. Trying to take care of things while he's away, eh?"

The Chief didn't wait for an answer. "Where's the rest of your gang?"

Christopher gulped. "Out back in the tree, I guess," he said and then added quickly, "sir."

The Chief jerked his thumb in the direction of the rowboat.

"Can we get there in this?" he asked.

"Yes, sir," Christopher answered eagerly. *"Yes, sir."*

He rowed the Chief and Jane to the back yard while Ann trailed along on shore with the baby carriage.

They had tied up the boat and were walking toward the tree when they heard the voice. Clearly it was Captain Happy's. It was booming from Timothy's radio, interrupted now and then by a sputter of static.

"Blowing up a bit out here," the voice said. "May run into some rough weather ahead. Not worried yet, though. Right now I'm digging into some clam chowder. On my third bowl."

Christopher wanted to listen to what Captain Happy was saying. He'd been looking forward to it all day and had meant to be home by four o'clock. Now that he was home, he had the Chief of Police along, glowering up at the tree and tapping his billy club impatiently.

"Timothy!" Christopher shouted into the tree. "Patrick! Mary! Come down here."

"Keep quiet," Timothy called back impatiently.

"Timothy," Christopher called desperately, "you've got to come."

"Shut up," Timothy yelled.

Patrick poked his head over a branch to look down. His eyes bulged.

"Timothy," he said in a resounding whisper, "we really do have to. It's the *Chief of Police!*"

"*Shut up!*"

Christopher jumped. This time it wasn't Timothy at all. It was the Chief. He had settled himself into Captain Happy's deck chair and had folded his hands over his stomach.

"Be quiet," he grunted. "Want to hear what the captain has to say."

Jane, Ann, and Christopher sat down on the ground. Captain Happy's voice continued.

"Have a new cook this trip," it went on. "Name is Spud. He can toss griddle cakes with both hands at the same time and not miss a one. Regular juggler, he is. What Spud cooks smells so good, we have fish for miles around following us just for a sniff!"

From under the tree the Chief chuckled. He took his hat off, dropped it on the ground, and stretched out in the deck chair.

"Speaking of food," Captain Happy's voice went on, "reminds me. There's a box of salt water taffy on the second shelf of the linen closet. Why don't you help yourself and pass it around?"

Christopher was about to leap to his feet but he remembered the Chief. Maybe this wasn't the time to think about candy.

The Chief glared at him. "Well," he roared, "you heard what the man said. Get going."

When Christopher came back with the taffy, the Chief of Police had his shoes off and was wiggling his toes in the grass. Captain Happy had gone off the air with the promise that he would be on again at ten o'clock the next morning. He couldn't talk longer now, he had explained, because of the wind. It had blown up so strong, the radio was needed for weather reports.

Timothy snapped off his set and followed the others down the tree. They lined up in front of the Chief of Police. . . .

"Ahem," the Chief began. He couldn't seem to think why the children were there until he caught sight of Ann's baby carriage parked under the tree.

The Chief tucked his stockinged feet under the chair.

"I don't want to see that monkey up street again," he said. "Ever. Especially in the Five and Ten. Understand?"

"Yes, sir," they answered together.

The Chief pulled his feet back out.

"That's all I have to say," he grunted, "but I could use a piece of taffy."

Christopher passed around the salt water taffy and then went up to the squirrel hole and produced orange pop. Jane and Mary agreed that from now on they would take turns feeding Jib so that Ann would have a rest. Then they all talked about Captain Happy and Spud and the weather at sea. They were having such a good time, they didn't notice the black clouds gathering.

All of a sudden the Chief's hat rolled away from his chair, and in the same breath two of Ann's hammocks were blown inside out.

"Whew!" the Chief exclaimed. "Blowing up a bit here too."

Jane glanced at the barometer.

"Oh, look!" she cried. "Look!"

The barometer had dropped fast. Right now it stood at a point that could mean only one thing—hurricane.

Chapter 12

"POOH!" Christopher scoffed. "Bet that old barometer is broken. Don't pay any attention to it. Let's pass around the taffy again."

But Timothy had already bounded up to the top of the tree and turned on the radio, tuning in on the middle of a sentence.

"—heading north at twenty-three miles an hour," the voice on the radio said. "The center of the hurricane is expected to stay out at sea but the edges will hit land sometime during the night."

"Pooh!" Christopher scoffed again. "What station have you got? Some old junky place down in Florida, probably."

"Florida, nothing!" Timothy called down impatiently. "It must be close—the barometer says so too." Already he was lowering his sail and packing up his radio.

In a minute, Christopher thought, he'll be telling everyone what to do. He'll be the captain of a ship in distress and all we'll hear will be that silly, navy, "sixteen-hundred" kind of talk!

And sure enough, there he went! "Clear the decks down below," Timothy called in a clipped voice of command. "Remove or secure all movable objects."

Christopher looked up at the sky. It had been cloudy most of the day, and now there were a few more gray clouds, a little wind—that was all. But Jane was helping Ann pack up her dolls. Mary was clearing out her desk and Patrick was unbuckling his saddle. Even the Chief of Police had tied up his shoelaces and hurried off at the first alarm. Phooy. Christopher took another piece of taffy and slammed the lid onto the box as Timothy became more and more captainish.

"Step lively now," Timothy barked. "On the double. Batten down the hatches."

"Aw, batten down your trap," Christopher grumbled. "I'm going home and get a weather report from a radio station I know something about." He turned on his heel and ambled off.

Five minutes later, when Christopher came out of the door of his house, he was carrying a large cardboard carton. "Got to pack up my jars," he mumbled to himself and he started to run. Then just as suddenly he slowed down. He was in no hurry to see Timothy right now, he remembered. And yet, after what he had just heard over his own radio, what else could he do? He quickened his pace again. Might as well get it over with, he thought, as he started up the tree with the carton.

Christopher left it on his counter, anchoring it against the wind with a pop bottle. He went on up the tree to the crow's nest, where Timothy was unscrewing his mast.

Christopher swallowed hard. "First mate reporting to the captain for orders, sir," he said clearly and crisply. "Wind from south at twenty knots. Due to arrive tonight at eleven." He hesitated while he did some fast figuring. "I mean," he corrected himself, "due to arrive at twenty-three hundred."

Timothy smiled. "I was waiting for your return, officer, to issue the final order."

Timothy jerked the mast free from the tree, put it under one arm, and cupped his hands to his mouth.

"All hands on deck!" he called. "Prepare to abandon ship."

Christopher scrambled down to the squirrel hole and with one sweep of his arm, tumbled his jars into the carton.

"I'll help you with that," Timothy said as he swung down from the crow's nest. He handed his mast and sail over to Patrick who, having taken care of his saddle long ago, was empty-handed.

Everyone else was out of the tree and waiting while Timothy and Christopher shuffled the carton awkwardly from branch to branch. When they were almost down, Timothy started to drop to the ground, but Christopher stopped him.

"Wait a minute," he said. "Let me go first."

Timothy threw his leg back over the branch. "For Pete's sake!" he exclaimed. "Why are you so special?" But he held onto the carton just the same.

Christopher jumped and came to attention on the ground below Timothy. "Because," he explained, "it is customary for the captain to be the last to leave a sinking ship." Christopher answered Timothy's embarrassed grin with a wide smile. "Am I correct, sir?"

"You are," Timothy laughed. "And now let's get these blasted rations of yours out of here and get going."

But now they were out of the tree, Timothy didn't feel much like a captain, after all. It was one thing to pretend in a tree boat, but another on solid ground with real responsibility ahead. What about the Raisin? What precautions should they take there?

Timothy looked over at the canal. "Someone better beach the rowboat," he suggested. His voice didn't sound captainish now, Christopher noticed, as he and Jane ran to the boat.

They were dragging it up onto the Buffalo dock when Wallie appeared. He hadn't bothered to tinkle the bell on his truck, or, if he had, they hadn't heard it above the wind.

"Better turn that boat over," Wallie advised,

running up to lend a hand. "Bottom up—that's it. Where's Timothy?"

"Why, he was right—" Christopher began, motioning toward the tree. But no one was there now. "He

must have gone inside." An arm shot out of an upstairs window of the Raisin and pulled a shutter closed. "There he is." Christopher pointed. "Locking the shutters. We better help."

Inside the Raisin everyone was acting fast. Patrick was winding the clock. Mary was watering her plants and Ann was giving Jib two extra bananas.

"You'll be all right," she told him. "And tomorrow I'll dress you up in baby clothes again."

"Better put him in his cage tonight," Wallie called as he locked the last of the downstairs shutters. "Hey, you guys upstairs—need any help?"

Timothy and Christopher clattered down the steps. "All done up there," Timothy reported. "Now what?"

Wallie put his hands on his hips and looked around. Jib and Porthole were caged and fed. The windows were protected. The lifesavers on the front of the house had been brought in.

"I think that does it," Wallie decided. "Nothing more we can do. Let's lock up and go."

The others started toward the front door, but Timothy made no move to follow.

"Come on," Patrick urged. "It's raining."

"You go ahead. I'll be along." Timothy continued to pace restlessly around the room.

Wallie shook his head firmly. "No," he declared. "When we go, we all go. What's the matter, Timothy?"

Timothy ran his fingers through his hair. "It's just that I won't know if everything is all right over here," he said unhappily. "I can't see the Raisin from my house at all."

"You couldn't do much about it anyway," Wallie reminded him.

"I'd *know*, though," Timothy insisted. "That's all. I'd just *know*."

"Well, for Pete's sake," Christopher groaned. "Is that all that's eating you? I'll let you know, Timothy. I'll call you up."

The answer was so simple, Christopher wondered why Timothy hadn't thought of it himself. Christopher's house, diagonally across the street from the Raisin, had a direct view of it. It was the only one on the street that did have. It would be easy to let Timothy know every hour on the hour what was happening.

But Timothy shook his head. "Good idea, Chris, but it won't work. The first thing to go out in a real hurricane is the telephone. Then the electric lights."

Patrick glanced uneasily up at the ceiling where the lights were still on. "I don't see why we're all talking," he shouted. "I don't see why we're not home."

"Wait a minute," Jane said. "I have an idea. What did people do before there were electric lights and telephones?" She spaced her words slowly and carefully. "What did Paul Revere do?"

"*I don't care what Paul Revere did,*" Patrick roared.

"He used secret signals," Jane went on, ignoring

Patrick. "And so will we. Candles. One candle in the window means something has happened at the Raisin. Two candles will mean it is more serious. Three candles will mean something terrible has happened."

Christopher's face lighted up. "You mean, I'll keep night watch. I'll light a candle in my room so Timothy can see it in his house."

Already Jane was over at a Weak Fish chest, pulling out the two dozen candles she had so recently scolded Captain Happy for buying.

"We'll all keep watch," she said. "Each of us has a bedroom window in sight of at least one other person's bedroom window. If Christopher lights a candle, Timothy can see it across the street and he'll light one in his window. I can see Timothy's window, so I'll light one and Patrick will see mine. The signal will go on like that, zigzag down the street. Mary will see Patrick's window and Ann will see Mary's. Ann won't need any candles because she's at the end of the line and won't need to signal anyone. Of course, if nothing happens, and it probably won't, no one will light any candles at all."

Jane distributed the candles—three to each, except Ann. "For a girl," Timothy admitted, as Jane gave him his candles, "you come up with some pretty good ideas."

Even Patrick seemed happier as they went out of the Raisin.

"I remember Paul Revere now," Jane heard him say softly to himself. "He rode a horse too."

Everyone was safe in his own house and supper was over before the wind began to show off in earnest. Suddenly it slapped the back of Christopher's house, walked around and pounced on the side of Patrick's. It roared down chimneys and rattled at doors. With his nose against his window, Christopher watched the wind whip off leaves, snap at twigs and then, as it roared on to hurricane size, go after whole branches.

At seven-thirty Mary saw the young birch tree in front of her house ripped up and flung across the sidewalk.

Eight o'clock. Bedtime started to roll up Pudding Street, beginning in Ann's room. But tonight, as soon as her light was off, Ann was up again in her pajamas. She stationed Lisa at one window and she took another.

Eight-thirty. Christopher picked up the telephone receiver to call Timothy. There was no sound—not even a crackle. The telephone was not working.

Nine o'clock. Bedtime swung up to Timothy's end of the street. Lights were snapped off in all upstairs windows. The real watch had begun!

Nine-thirty. The street lights blinked off and all the downstairs windows were suddenly dark. The electricity had gone off. One by one, dots of candlelight appeared in windows downstairs. But upstairs, every window remained as black as the night itself.

Behind his window, Christopher's eyes were fixed on the Raisin. He watched the rain lash it and the wind whirl around it, but there was nothing to report. The Raisin stood strong.

Ten o'clock. Christopher was growing sleepy. If only he had a bottle of pop to drink, maybe he could stay awake. He thought about sneaking downstairs, but he didn't dare leave the window. Every now and then there seemed to be a queer noise behind the roaring of the wind.

Flap, flap. Christopher peered into the darkness. There it was—a shutter at the Raisin, swinging back and forth, clattering and banging against the house. Suddenly it ripped loose and soared off into space. It wasn't anything to worry about, Christopher knew, yet he did think it was worth one candle.

And so the first upstairs candle was lit—one little prick of light, winking its message across Pudding Street: "Something has happened at the Raisin. Not much, but something." Like a zigzag chain, four other lights immediately followed.

Christopher smiled as he saw Timothy's candle and pictured the other candles down the street. Everyone was depending on *him,* he thought, and he stared harder than ever into the night. But there was nothing to see. His eyes ached from straining through the dark and also, he admitted, from plain sleepiness. If he lay down for a few minutes, he would be able to hear anything that happened. A hurricane seemed to be something to hear rather than to see, anyway.

Christopher stretched out on his bed and closed his eyes. The hurricane was coming now in regular gusts, like a kind of howling music. He could count out the time just as he did when he played his bugle. One, two, three, four—*BLOW*. One, two, three . . . Christopher was asleep.

A few minutes later Christopher's mother and father decided to go to bed, too. Each holding a candle, they felt their way upstairs and stopped at Christopher's room.

His mother put her candle down on the window sill beside Christopher's candle. "I'll fix his covers," she whispered to his father, "while you check on the windows."

Christopher's father added his candle to the two already on the window sill.

Across the street, Timothy could hardly believe his eyes. Three candles—what could it mean?

Something terrible . . . something terrible . . . The news sped down the street.

Timothy sat on the edge of his bed with his head in his hands. What could have happened? Could the roof have blown off? Could the tree have blown over?

Timothy was putting into words some of the pos-

189

sibilities that he had not dared even to think about. His real fear, that all evening he had been trying to hide even from himself, came stalking out into the open.

What about the captain?

Timothy remembered the radio broadcast . . . "the center of the hurricane is expected to stay out at sea . . ."

What part of the sea? he asked himself. How did a ship manage in the center of a hurricane? Was the captain in danger at this very minute?

Timothy got up and paced his room, trying to shake off some of his worry. He looked out of his window. Across the street Christopher's candles were out and his room was dark. Timothy decided that he might as well blow his out too. The candles had told the news by now. With one breath he blew them out and watched to see Jane do the same.

Now that the street was dark, the wind sounded wilder than ever, as if it should have been roaring through African jungles or around Arctic icebergs rather than wasting its time on such a little place as Pudding Street. Timothy shivered and tossed restlessly on his bed.

What could have happened?

The same question was whirling all the way down Pudding Street, except, of course, in Christopher's house. He slept peacefully through the night and never heard the message that seemed to be on the very lips of the wind, Mary thought—"something terrible, terrible."

Never had morning seemed so long in coming. When it finally did come, Timothy had fallen to sleep in spite of himself. The first thing he noticed when he woke up was a patch of sunlight on his bed. He leaped up and put on his dungarees.

Jane, Patrick, Mary, and Ann were already at the Raisin when Timothy got there. Jane shrugged her shoulders as Timothy ran up.

"We can't find a thing," she said. "We've been all around. Everything seems to be all right."

At first glance, the Raisin certainly looked as solid as ever. Its roof was intact, its chimneys standing. It was true that an upstairs shutter lay on the ground and another hung by one hinge. The canal was flooded, but that wasn't serious.

Timothy went around to the back to look at the tree. He expected broken twigs and scattered leaves but, even so, he hadn't known quite how it would feel to see the tree stripped so bare. Most of the leaves were gone and those that still clung to the branches were brown and papery. As Timothy looked up into the tree, he could see his deck plainly. It had held together fine. In fact, on closer observation, Timothy could see that no real damage at all had been done in the tree. Then what had Christopher meant?

Timothy turned to go in search of him, but Christopher was already standing right there with a broad grin on his face.

"We weathered it pretty well, didn't we?" Christopher asked.

"Then what was the big idea?" Timothy shouted. "Three candles!"

"Three!" Christopher repeated blankly. "What are you talking about? I only lit one."

"Oh, sure!" Everyone joined in now, accusing Christopher—all but Patrick. He stood at the edge of the circle, scuffing the ground with the toe of his shoe. Timothy looked just the way he had the day he had been mad about the canal. It gave Patrick a hollow feeling in his stomach.

"Maybe Christopher really didn't," he managed to say at last, and as the others turned to listen to him, he went on more bravely, "Maybe he went to sleep. Maybe his mother put those candles there."

Christopher was staring at the ground. "I did go to sleep," he admitted. "I didn't mean to."

He looked so sorry that Patrick jammed his hands into his pockets and strode over beside him. He set his legs solidly apart and glared at everyone else.

"Of course he couldn't help it," he said loudly. *"Even Paul Revere went to sleep sometimes."*

The hard, straight line of Timothy's mouth relaxed and then turned into a grin. "Thought you were the fellow who didn't care what Paul Revere did," he said.

· "The main thing," Patrick declared happily, "is that the Raisin is safe."

Timothy looked at his watch. Two more hours until time to turn on the radio.

"The main thing is," he told himself quietly, "how is Captain Happy?"

Chapter 13

BY TEN O'CLOCK Timothy had the radio rigged up again in the crow's nest and everyone was gathered anxiously around as he prepared to tune in.

Timothy looked at his watch. "It's time," he said. His mouth felt dry and crackly when he spoke. He switched on the radio and turned the dial quickly to the proper place.

But there wasn't a sound.

"Maybe it hasn't had time to warm up yet," Jane suggested.

Timothy nodded silently and they waited. Still nothing happened. Timothy turned the dial a little to the left and there was a blare of rhumba music. Quickly he turned the dial back, but after the music, the tree seemed quieter than before.

"Maybe your watch is wrong," Mary said.

Timothy shook his head. He had checked it before he came up the tree. He felt a pounding in his throat as he twisted the dial this way and that, tuning in easily on other ships at sea but never on the Steamer *Merryweather*. Never on Captain Happy.

At ten-thirty when the radio still remained silent, Jane suggested they turn it off and try again at four o'clock.

"Turn it off?" Timothy echoed. "Are you crazy? I'm going to leave this radio on and stay right here until, until . . ." Until Captain Happy *does* come on, Timothy was about to say, but he was stopped by a faint coughing from the radio.

With trembling hands, Timothy reached over to check the dial again. Yes, it was at the right place. He leaned forward tensely to catch any further sound and was all but blasted out of the tree by the crackle that followed. For a full minute the crackle continued and then turned gradually into a howl, then into a roar. And finally the booming voice of Captain Happy burst into the air.

"Are you still there, Timothy?" it called. "Are you there?"

"Yes," Ann called back loudly but she was quickly hushed by the others.

"In case you are there," Captain Happy went on, "I'll apologize for being late. Just plain overslept—that's all."

Timothy slumped with relief.

"Missed out on a mess of griddle cakes, too," Captain Happy went on with a chuckle, "but I'll make up for it. Trouble with me was I stayed up most of the night playing tag with a hurricane. Must have been so frazzled this morning, they all let me sleep through. At breakfast time, my eyes were closed tighter than an oyster shell." Captain Happy paused.

"Did your boat get hurt?" Ann shouted, still convinced that if she could hear Captain Happy, he must be able to hear her, too. And as if to answer her question, he continued.

"Everything shipshape this morning. Got slapped around last night but stood it stoutly. No damage and clear sailing ahead. The water is still choppy but the sky this morning is as blue as—"

Captain Happy hesitated and Mary pictured him squinting up into the blue as he looked for a word.

"As blue as Mary's eyes," he concluded. Mary smiled and felt her cheeks grow warm. "Have a feeling the whole world is catching its breath. How about you?"

"We're all right," Ann shouted, glaring right back at Timothy. He didn't seem to want her to say *anything*.

Then Captain Happy was signing off. "I'll talk to you this afternoon. And you won't catch me napping again," he laughed.

As Timothy snapped off the radio, the top of the tree exploded into a shout of joy. Patrick cut loose with a series of Indian war whoops so curdling no one could help joining in. At last, exhausted and out of breath, they dropped to the ground. Only Timothy stayed in the crow's nest a moment longer. He stretched himself tall and sent up his private war whoop into the sky which sounded, even Timothy had to admit, more like a rooster than an Indian. Anyway, what better place to crow than a crow's nest?

"I feel so good," he cried, "—bet I could fly!"

Lying on the ground under the tree, Christopher turned over on his back and looked up.

"Well, don't try it, Superman," he warned. "Just come down the regular way. We've got work to do."

Timothy looked down at the ground. All around the Raisin and under the tree was a litter of leaves and twigs and papers strewn by the wind. He had hardly noticed before how mussed up Pudding Street was, but the mess didn't bother him. It would be fun to clean up. Anything would be fun today. Captain Happy was safe!

"Watch out down below!" Timothy sang out and swung himself down the tree from branch to branch, making a perfect landing with one foot neatly in the middle of Christopher's stomach.

"Ugh," Christopher groaned and then raised himself on one elbow. "Listen, if you have so much energy, you clean up. We'll watch."

A few minutes later they all had rakes and brooms and were attacking the rubbish left by the hurricane.

They had cleaned up around the front of the house and had made several great piles of leaves behind the Raisin when Mary leaned on her rake and looked up at the tree.

"It's so bare now without the leaves," she sighed. "It looks undressed."

"It will take some getting used to," Jane agreed, "but the climbing will be just as good. And next spring we'll have leaves again."

She tossed her rake on the ground and dropped down to rest beside the largest pile of leaves. She was still thinking about the tree, so she didn't notice the faint stirring in the leaves.

Scrounged down at the bottom of the leaf pile close to Jane, Patrick was trying not to make even the slightest movement. He was hiding, waiting for someone to say, "Why, where's Patrick?" He wouldn't come out the first time anyone said it; he would wait until they were all saying it. Then he would erupt like a volcano from the mountain of leaves. It was certainly about time for someone to start missing him, he thought impatiently.

"Patrick's leafy place is gone now," Christopher was saying.

Now they would notice. Patrick set himself for a leap.

But they were talking about the tree again.

"With the leaves gone," Timothy was saying, "we're more out in the public. Maybe we should make some winter improvements."

"Like putting up storm windows, I suppose," Christopher grunted. There was a pause before he went on. "We do seem to be closer to each other than we used to be."

Down in the leaf pile, Patrick blew a piece of twig out of his mouth. He was getting pretty tired of all this *yakety-yak* business above him. You would think someone would *notice*. Now there was Ann talking.

"I think we're much too close," Ann said importantly. "I'm going to hang curtains around my living room. I don't want to be so near that old Lickety."

At that moment the volcano exploded. The mountain split apart and Patrick's face—red, dirty, and angry—glared out from among the leaves.

"What's the matter with Lickety?" he shouted.

Ann seemed to be neither surprised nor interested in Patrick's sudden appearance. She tilted her nose daintily into the air.

"Horses smell," she said.

Patrick's eyes bulged. His cheeks puffed out, and for a moment he couldn't seem to do anything but sputter. Mary felt sorry for him. He was having such trouble finding words that were strong enough.

Finally he opened his mouth and shouted at the top of his lungs.

"Lickety does not smell." He marched over to Ann, who had turned her back and was pretending that the conversation between Patrick and herself was finished.

"I don't think Captain Happy is going to like the tree," Ann said thoughtfully, but no one was listening to her.

"Don't change the subject," Patrick roared. "Lickety does *not* smell."

Mary put her hand on Patrick's arm. "Of course, he doesn't," she agreed gently, trying to think how all this had started. She remembered Patrick bursting out of the leaves.

"Say, Patrick," Mary said, *"where were you?* For the longest time I was wondering where you were."

Patrick turned around quickly to face Mary. "Huh?" he said blankly.

"Where were you? We couldn't imagine where you had gone. We missed you."

Patrick pointed with satisfaction at the leaf pile. "I was right there. All the time, I was right there. Guess I had you worried." He dropped happily to the ground with the others.

Ann turned around to face the group again. Now maybe she could say what she had been trying to say for the last five minutes.

"I don't think Captain Happy is going to like the tree," she repeated primly. "I think we should decorate it. So it will look nice when he first comes home and he can get used to the leaves being off."

Patrick snorted. Any idea Ann would have couldn't possibly be any good. He wasn't going to pay any attention to her. But he noticed that everyone else was looking thoughtful. Mary's eyes were sparkling.

"We can have a coming-home party for Captain Happy," she said. "And the decorated tree will be part of the celebration."

"And refreshments," Christopher added happily.

"And poetry," Mary continued. "It will be better than any christening party we ever had and we have a whole tree to decorate."

The idea *was* beginning to sound good.

"What are we going to use for decorations?" Patrick asked.

Timothy remembered the Christmas box he had raided to decorate his platform at the christening of the Raisin. If it were only Christmas, it would be easy to decorate the tree. That reminded him—what was the exact date Captain Happy was due home?

"Let's see now," he said, "Captain Happy will be back ten days from August 25. That makes it . . ."

Mary had already climbed up the tree and was looking at her desk calendar. "September 5," she called down, "Labor Day!"

"Hurrah!" Patrick shouted. "We'll have a Labor Day tree."

"And what," Christopher asked with exaggerated politeness, "if I may be bold enough to inquire—is a Labor Day tree?"

Patrick thought fast. He had never been sure just what it was that Labor Day celebrated. He guessed there wasn't any special kind of decorations for it.

"Well, a Labor Day tree," he began vaguely, "is a tree . . . er . . . um . . . that you labor especially hard to decorate. You just don't put on Christmas decorations or Easter decorations or anything that easy." Patrick warmed to his subject and went on enthusiastically. "No. On a Labor Day tree you have to put on decorations for every holiday in the year. It's the hardest kind of tree to trim. Takes real labor. That's why it's called a Labor Day tree. Get it?"

Christopher grinned. "I get it."

"I think it's a wonderful idea!" Mary exclaimed. "I want to make the valentine decorations."

"I'll color Easter eggs to hang on the tree," Jane volunteered. Christopher and Timothy offered to supply Christmas decorations, and Patrick said he would bring flags and red, white, and blue streamers for the Fourth of July.

"I guess there's nothing left for you, Ann," Patrick said, not sounding too unhappy about it.

Ann was on her feet and starting home.

"Oh, yes," she contradicted him. "Halloween. I am very good at making orange jack-o'-lanterns."

All week the boys and girls of Pudding Street made and gathered decorations for the Labor Day tree. Jane insisted that her family have scrambled eggs for breakfast, and every morning she got up early to blow out the eggs so that she could have the empty shells to paint. By Labor Day morning she had twenty-six painted eggs.

Mary had made twenty large valentines with paper lace trimming—each one with a different greeting for Captain Happy. The one she liked best was,

From the briny deep
Where'er you roam,
We wish to welcome you
Back home.

She was particularly pleased with "briny" and "where'er." They were words she didn't have a chance to use just any day in the week.

They didn't dare, of course, to decorate the tree ahead of time.

"If it rains, we'll just have to forget the tree," Jane said.

It didn't rain. Labor Day morning was clear and lovely, with just a hint of fall crispness to the air. Mary hung a valentine on the end of a branch and noticed that already Christopher and Timothy had hung over half of their Christmas balls. The trimming was going surprisingly fast. They had worked so hard all week on the decorations, yet when they came to put them up, there didn't seem to be very many. Patrick and Ann had their flags and jack-o'-lanterns up in a few minutes, and the valentines and Easter eggs took only a little longer.

They stepped back to look at the final effect.

The tree still looked bare. True, there were gay spots scattered here and there, but the tree didn't look trimmed.

"It looks as if we started to decorate it," Mary said disappointedly, "but got tired and never finished."

And there was no time to make anything more. Captain Happy was due soon, and they still had to get the refreshments together.

Mary had to finish the poem she was writing in honor of Captain Happy's return. She sat working, under the tree, rather than at her desk, so that she wouldn't get mixed up with the decorations. She moistened the tip of her pencil on her tongue. What she had already written sounded all right, but she couldn't seem to finish it off.

> Pudding Street is glad to say
> That Captain Happy's home today.
> Our jobs we've done with utmost care
> In weather foul and weather fair.
> Porthole, Jib, the fish are fine.
> Your wooden Indian is well shined.
> The rugs are brushed, the clock is wound,
> The plants are watered all around . . .

Now this was the part that was hard. Mary had wanted to report on all the jobs, but she hadn't mentioned the tandem bicycle yet.

"We've oiled and ridden the tandem bicycle," she wrote and stopped. What could rhyme with bicycle? Tricycle, icicle . . . She couldn't use those words. "Tricycle, icicle . . ." Mary jumped. "Icicle, icicle," she cried and rushed into the Raisin.

When she came out, she was carrying the enormous box that had been put away long ago in a

Weak Fish chest—the box of red and white plastic icicles.

"For the tree," she explained happily. "They'll be perfect."

The icicles were just what they needed. There were hundreds of them. Everyone set to work. They started at the top and worked down, leaving the tree shimmering magically in the sunlight. When they stood back to look at it this time, they smiled with satisfaction.

"That's what a Labor Day tree is supposed to look like," Patrick declared in an official voice.

Mary sat down to write the last lines of her poem.

> We've oiled and ridden the tandem bicycle,
> We've hung the tree with plastic icicles.
> We hope you like what we have done.
> We think it's been a lot of fun.

Chapter 14

CHRISTOPHER COLUMBUS!" Captain Happy cried as he sailed around the house and saw the tree. The boys and girls of Pudding Street gathered close and glowed with pride.

"It's a Labor Day tree," Patrick explained.

"Decorated for you," Mary said.

"And I thought of it," Ann added, holding tight to Captain Happy's hand.

Captain Happy walked around the tree, looking at it from all sides. His smile grew broader and broader as Patrick, who had appointed himself official guide, pointed out valentines, jack-o'-lanterns, flags, eggs, and Christmas balls.

"I see my icicles came in handy," Captain Happy chuckled as he completed his tour around the tree. He put his hands in his pockets and leaned back on his heels.

"Never," he said, *"never* in all my travels have I seen a sight so beautiful."

He went on looking and looking, saying nothing, and rocking back and forth on his heels in wonder.

On the tree the icicles tinkled merrily in the breeze.

Christopher was as happy as everyone else, but he had had enough of looking at the tree. His mouth was beginning to ache from smiling so long. He moved about uneasily, waiting for someone to say something and go on with the program. Finally he cleared his throat abruptly.

"We've got eats, too," he said.

Jane glared at him. "We promised to wait for Wallie before beginning that," she said.

At last Captain Happy turned away from the tree.

"Come along to the car and help me unload," he said, tapping Christopher on the shoulder. "I have some things to contribute to this home-coming too."

When he and Christopher came back, each had a bulging duffel bag. Captain Happy carried his slung over his shoulder like a pack and he was laughing loudly at something Christopher had said.

"Ho, ho, ho!" he roared.

Ann looked up, startled.

"Now I know," she said slowly. Captain Happy had always reminded her of someone, but she never could think who it was.

"You are just like Santa Claus," she declared. "I bet you're a relation."

Captain Happy laughed harder than ever. "No," he admitted finally between gasps.

Ann's eyes were fixed firmly on Captain Happy's middle.

"You are, too," she insisted. "I can tell. It shakes when you laugh like a bowlful of jelly."

Captain Happy clutched his stomach. "Oh, no!"

he howled. He pulled such a comical face he had everyone, even Ann, laughing with him.

Captain Happy sat down and took Ann onto his lap.

"Not even distantly related," he told her. "All my relatives are weak fish."

He opened his duffel bag and turned it upside down. A mountain of cellophane-wrapped candy canes and popcorn balls tumbled out onto the grass.

"Weak fish, nothing!" Christopher exclaimed excitedly. "*That* was no weak fish buy!" He picked up a popcorn ball and noticed a little loop of string at the end of the cellophane. "Look!" he said. "All ready to hang on the tree until such time"—he glanced at Jane—"as we can eat them."

Everyone had a hand in hanging up popcorn and candy canes. When the tree was loaded, they piled what was left over with the picnic supplies on the blankets Christopher had spread under the tree.

Captain Happy opened the other bag.

"Don't believe I was such a weak fish here either," he said.

He handed a small dancing doll to Ann, a compass to Timothy, a pair of spurs to Patrick. He reached his hand in again and pulled out a fingerprinting set for Jane and a book of poetry for Mary. Down deep in the bag were several lumpy shapes that Christopher had had his eye on right from the beginning. Captain Happy pulled out one of them. It was a fresh coconut for Christopher. He reached down again and came up with a fresh pineapple.

"Also for Christopher. And that's all," Captain Happy said. "Was I a weak fish this trip?"

"No!" It was a loud, unanimous, happy chorus.

As Christopher rattled his coconut at his ear, he

glanced at the duffel bag Captain Happy was closing. There still seemed to be some lumpy shapes at the bottom of it.

"Emptied your bags, did you?" Christopher asked innocently.

Captain Happy looked at the lumpy shapes. "Just about," he said and stopped. "Might as well show you the worst," he said shamefacedly. He turned the bag upside down and out fell an assortment of ash trays, soap dishes, pincushions, and glasses cases.

Christopher was about to say something, but he was stopped by Ann.

"Don't you dare," she said fiercely. "You can't scold a relative of Santa Claus, no matter what he buys."

Christopher agreed. Besides, there was something more important to do. Wallie's bell was tinkling in front of the Raisin.

"Let's eat!" Christopher cried happily.

But just as he started to open up the picnic supplies, Wallie dashed around the side of the Raisin and motioned him to wait.

"Not yet," Wallie said. "I think we're going to have company."

"Who?"

Wallie smiled mysteriously. "Wait and see. As a matter of fact, you'll hear before you see."

From the other end of Pudding Street there was a burst of music. That couldn't be company, but

Patrick ran out onto the sidewalk anyway. When he came back, his face was a-glow.

"It's the Chief of Police," he shouted, "and the whole village band!"

All the way down Pudding Street the band came. It turned in at the Raisin and marched right through the yard. The wind instruments came along one side of the canal and the drums the other. They met at Buffalo, wheeled sharply, and headed straight toward the captain. A few yards away from him, they stopped and the Chief of Police strode out in front to shake hands with Captain Happy.

"Welcome home," he said formally, then punched Captain Happy in the ribs, "you old sardine."

When the Chief and Captain Happy at last seemed to have finished slapping each other on the back, Christopher coughed loudly from among the picnic supplies.

"You look weak, boy," Captain Happy said. "You need nourishment."

He walked out to his car and came back, rolling a barrel of Spud's cookies.

"Dig in," he cried as he flung off the lid.

Wallie's ice cream, Spud's cookies, and Captain Happy's popcorn balls stretched Christopher's refreshments into a feast. Everyone sat on the ground, ate, and told jokes. Patrick went from one drum to another, rolling out magnificent noises. But every once in a while the drummers would take back their

sticks and the band would break into a song that
seemed to make all the men smile.

"What's that song they keep playing?" Christopher asked the Chief.

"It's an old-time one," the Chief said. "Happy
Days Are Here Again."

After that, the band played "Anchors Aweigh"
and all the other sea songs they knew. Mary recited
her poem. Then just as the band was ready to leave,
Jane reached into the pocket of her dress and
brought out a big, red firecracker.

"This is the right time," she announced.

She set it carefully on the Buffalo dock. She bor-
rowed a match from Captain Happy and ordered
everyone to stand back. She went through every motion slowly, knowing that this was the last firecracker
of the year. She lit it.

BOOM BAH

"Best Fourth of July firecracker I ever heard on
Labor Day," the Chief of Police declared as the band
marched away down Pudding Street.

Back at the tree, both food and talk seemed to
have dwindled. Captain Happy, Wallie, and the boys
and girls of Pudding Street sprawled happily on the
ground, thinking over what a fine day it had been.

"If only it could always be like this," Christopher
thought, "all of us together, the tree, plenty of
food . . ."

He stirred uncomfortably as thoughts of the future crowded out the present. Time was speeding ahead far too fast. Right now Christopher was not eager for time to move ahead at all. Certainly not into the next day. Tomorrow everything would change.

"Suppose you remember what happens tomorrow," he remarked gloomily. "School!" Christopher answered himself and sighed deeply. "Nothing will be the same."

Captain Happy glanced at the faces around him. They all looked as if they had suddenly been hit with wet washcloths.

"Come, come, now," Captain Happy laughed jovially. "Summer's not the only time for fun. The tree is going to stay right here, you know. I am, too, most of the time, and Wallie too, I bet."

But Wallie shook his head. "I'll be going back to college in another week," he said, "but I'll be back for holidays."

"Suppose you'll be putting the ice-cream truck up for the winter," Christopher said sadly.

"And shaving off your mustache," Jane added.

"Well, yes," Wallie admitted. "But the tree may be even more fun in winter."

"Aye," Captain Happy agreed. "It's when the wind changes that it often blows the best. You'll see."

Christopher grunted and retreated into his own

215

dreary thoughts. The breeze was blowing harder now, ringing the icicles on the tree together like bells.

"That's all we'll hear, beginning tomorrow," Christopher grumbled to himself. "Bells."

And as if to underline his gloom, a long, low, mournful honk sounded on Pudding Street. At first Christopher didn't pay much attention to it, but when it was repeated, he looked around at the others. Everyone was sitting up, alert, exchanging puzzled glances. Christopher frowned. There was something familiar about that honk. He had a vague, uneasy feeling that someone or something unpleasant was lurking just out of sight.

And then Miss Pursey rounded the corner of the Raisin, walking as briskly as if she had just stepped from the house. Behind her shuffled Mr. Shift.

The boys and girls of Pudding Street stared in horror as she stalked up to Captain Happy. Her mouth was set in the thin, grim line they remembered so well, as if she had buttoned it up for keeps with one of her own precious buttons. And now that she started to speak, she opened it no more than buttonhole width.

"Didn't care for the rest of the world," she announced. "Brought my buttons and came back. Would like to buy 121 now, even if it doesn't look the same." She sniffed with disapproval as she looked around.

216

Then she seemed to wait a moment before she went on to ask the question, the terrible question that now they all knew must come. The children watched Captain Happy carefully for the first weak fish symptoms. They tensed themselves and waited, ready to remind him with a stiff poke, to outshout him, or to do anything else the emergency might require. Christopher fingered his coconut and Patrick bared his teeth like a cross dog.

Miss Pursey looked directly at Captain Happy. "Will you sell the house?" she asked.

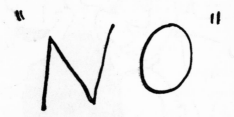

Captain Happy thundered it out before Miss Pursey had even quite finished with the question. Long before anyone could possibly have done any reminding.

"No, ma'am," he shouted. "No, indeed. No, thank you. I should say *not*. Under *no* circumstances."

Before Captain Happy had reached even the third No, Miss Pursey and Mr. Shift had disappeared. By the fourth No, everyone was clapping, dancing, laughing, hugging Captain Happy, slapping him on the back, shaking his hand. The fifth and sixth No's were muffled.

Captain Happy winked at Christopher. "Just as I

told you," he said, "you never can tell about the wind . . ."

All at once Christopher felt warm and happy right down to his bones. Not just the kind of happiness that comes with good news or a good meal. This was different.

Mary caught hold of Captain Happy's hand. Still fresh in her mind was the first line of the poem she had read at the party. Quickly she added another second line.

"Pudding Street is glad to say
That Captain Happy's here to stay."

"Captain Happy's here to stay!" They all picked up the last line and shouted it again.

"Let's have another pop!" Christopher said happily.